I0556390

Sin Eater

By John R. Schembra

Writers Exchange E-Publishing

http://www.writers-exchange.com

Sin Eater
Copyright 2016, 2025 John R. Schembra
Writers Exchange E-Publishing
PO Box 372
ATHERTON QLD 4883

Cover Art by: Jatin

Published by Writers Exchange E-Publishing
http://www.writers-exchange.com

ISBN: **ebook**: 978-1-925191-92-9
Print: 978-1-925191-92-9 (WEE Assigned)

The unauthorized reproduction or distribution of this copyrighted work is illegal. Criminal copyright infringement, including infringement without monetary gain, is investigated by the FBI and is punishable by up to 5 (five) years in federal prison and a fine of $250,000.

Names, characters and incidents depicted in this book are products of the author's imagination and are used fictitiously. Any resemblance to actual events, locales, organizations, or persons, living or dead, is entirely coincidental and beyond the intent of the author.

No part of this book may be reproduced or transmitted in any form or any means, electronic or mechanical, including photocopying, recording, or by any information storage and retrieval system, without permission from the publisher.

Contents

Prologue 1

Chapter 1 5

Chapter 2 12

Chapter 3 20

Chapter 4 26

Chapter 5 34

Chapter 6 40

Chapter 7 44

Chapter 8 52

Chapter 9 59

Chapter 10 64

Chapter 11 71

Chapter 12 77

Chapter 13 82

Chapter 14 88

Chapter 15 92

Chapter 16 97

Chapter 17 103

Chapter 18 107

Chapter 19 112

Chapter 20 118

Chapter 21 121

Chapter 22 125

Chapter 23 131

About the Author.. 136

An Echo of Lies 138

A Vince Torelli Novel 139

A Vince Torelli Mystery 140

Sin Eater 143

Sin Eater; In folklore, a person who would take on the sins of a dying person through ritual means and for material gain, thus absolving the dying of their sins while taking on the burden of the same.

Prologue

He clung tightly to his mother's hand as they walked down the dimly lit hallway toward the bedroom. He could hear the soft sobbing of his aunts in the living room, punctuated once in a while by a sharp wail, frightening him even more. He reached up with his other hand and held on to his mother with both of his as they approached the door, his heart thumping so hard in his chest he thought it would burst. They stopped at the closed door and his mother knelt down facing him. Placing her hands on his shoulders, she looked into his eyes, seeing his fear.

"Not to worry, Nico." She said, stroking his cheek gently. "It is natural that people pass on. Your granddad has been sick for a while now, and it is his time to leave. God is coming to take him to heaven soon, so we must go in and say our goodbyes." She smoothed his hair as she talked, her voice comforting. Though still afraid, her words took some of the fear from him. He nodded to her without speaking, afraid his voice would betray him. He wanted her to think he was brave, a big boy whom she could be proud of, not a frightened little six year old.

"Now, when we go in, Honey, don't be surprised at how Granddad looks. This disease has changed him, but know this, my son, it is still your granddad lying in that bed. Do not be afraid. He is still the same person who took you fishing. The same granddad that would play games with you, take you to the movies, help you with your homework, OK?"

He nodded again, a lump starting to form in his throat. He loved his grand-dad, and the time they spent together was some of his favorite time. He knew no father, as his dad left when he was just a baby. He understood what death was and knew that when his granddad died he would be gone forever, just like their cat that had died last year. He was trying his best not to cry, but he couldn't keep the tears from clouding his vision. He rubbed his eyes with the back of his hands, wiping away the tears that threatened to spill down his cheeks.

"I know, Honey," his mother said, gently squeezing his shoulder. "This is hard on you, but I know you want to say goodbye to him, to let him know you love him and will never forget him." Her voice caught in her throat and she took a slow, deep breath, willing herself to not cry in front of her son. Under control once more, she asked, "Are you ready, son?"

"Yes," he said so softly she had to lean in to hear him. She kissed him on the cheek and stood up. Taking his hand once more, she faced the door, took a deep breath, and opened it.

The room was dark, the only light coming from some candles on the nightstand next to the bed and on the dresser. It smelled musty and mediciney, almost unclean. He could see his grandmother sitting in a rocking chair next to the bed, holding the family bible on her lap. She had a shawl around her shoulders and her gray hair was pulled tightly back into a bun. Her head was resting against the back of the chair and her eyes were closed. She appeared to be asleep.

He couldn't see his granddad on the bed, only an un-recognizable form under the covers. He could hear him breathing, could hear the breath rattling in his throat as his body fought for air. His mother led him to the side of the bed opposite his grandmother.

"I'm glad you're here, Caroline. You too, Nico," his grandmother said without opening her eyes or lifting her head. A fleeting thought skipped through his mind. *How did she know it was us?* Just as quickly it was gone, unanswered.

"He was asking for you both just a few hours ago. I'm glad you got here in time."

"We drove on down just as soon as we could, Ma," his mother said in hushed tones, as if she was afraid of disturbing her father, lying so thin and pale on the bed. Nico hardly recognized his grandfather, he had lost so much weight.

"Shall we pray together, Ma?" his mother asked, kneeling at the bedside. She tugged on his coat and he, too, kneeled next to the bed. He was so small, he couldn't see over the mattress. As his mother and grandmother began to pray, he folded his hands together and bowed his head, not knowing the words but knowing they were important. When they were done, his mother got to her feet. Nico stood up and looked up at her, seeing the tears in her eyes. He saw her take his granddad's hand, pressing it to her cheek. She kissed it and said, "Goodbye, Pop. I love you." The tears were running freely down her cheeks now. He looked at his grandfather lying there so still and pale. He reached up and took his grandfather's hand from his mother, kissed it, too, and said, "Goodbye, granddad."

A soft knock on the doorjamb interrupted them. It was his great aunt Helen. "He's just arrived, Josie," she said to his grandmother. "Shall I have him come in?"

"Yes, Helen. I fear there is not much time left." His grandmother got up from the chair, placing the bible on the seat. She pulled the covers down to his grandfather's waist and folded them over. Nico could see his granddad was dressed in his best suit. His grandmother took a small plate from on top of the dresser and placed it on his chest. A small piece of bread was on the plate. He watched as she opened the top drawer of the dresser and took out a small cloth bag. Opening the bag, she took out two small gold coins and placed them on his granddads closed eyelids. Turning to her sister, she said, softly, "Bring him in, Helen."

His mother turned to her and said, "You really didn't call one, did you Ma?"

"Yes, Caroline, I did." She sighed and continued, "I know you don't believe in it, but I do, and so does your father. It is important to us. He asked for him, and I will honor his wishes."

"It's just an old superstition, Ma. It does no good, and I don't want some stranger coming in here and desecrating my father with this archaic ritual."

"You don't have any say in the matter, Caroline. It's what your father wanted. If you don't like it, don't want to see it, then wait in the parlor, but he is coming in."

"But Ma, a Sin Eater?"

"This conversation is over, Caroline," his grandmother said, folding her arms over her chest.

His mother sighed and shook her head. Taking his hand she said, "Come on, sweetheart. Let's go back to the living room."

As they turned to go, Nico saw a large figure blocking the doorway. He was wearing a black suit with a white dress shirt, a black tie and a black top hat. He carried a small, worn leather satchel in one hand and a cane in the other.

He had the most piercing eyes Nico had ever seen. They appeared to burn with a reddish color and seemed to look through him into his soul. Nico's gaze locked on the man's, and when the man smiled, a mirthless, humorless smile,

Nico could see his teeth were coated and yellowish. There were gaps where missing teeth had rotted out.

Nico suddenly felt dizzy. Shadows began to creep in from the edges of his vision, and he staggered slightly. He felt as if someone was pulling him into a dark place, a place of death and disease, a place that terrified him. He could feel a connection with the dark man, almost read his thoughts, and he shivered from the feeling of pure evil and degradation that came from him. His vision narrowed even more, and he felt the strength flowing from his body. It was getting harder and harder to move his arms or legs. It became difficult to breath and he felt as if he was drowning.

He felt someone shaking him, saying something, but it sounded like they were talking to him from far away. He was shaken harder, and recognized his mother's voice asking if he was all right. He broke eye contact with the man in black. The room came back into focus and his hearing cleared. He looked at his mother and blinked rapidly, then shook his head yes. His heart had begun to beat rapidly again, and he felt a fear so strong it was almost overwhelming. He felt sweat trickling down the back of his neck, and his body shook involuntarily. His mother, alarmed by his behavior, bent over and picked him up, carrying him rapidly past the man in black and out of the bedroom. He had his face buried in her shoulder so he couldn't see the man as they passed him. As his mother hurried down the hallway, he looked up and saw the man in black slowly closing the door. Just before the door closed, the man looked directly at him and winked.

Chapter 1

Nico frantically searched through the papers on his desk for the blank final exam. *Damn,* he thought, *where did I put it?* In his haste, several sheets fell to the floor. He bent over to pick them up and saw the exam he was looking for laying on top of the pile. *I have GOT to get more organized.* His office was no more than a cubicle. It was eight feet wide and ten feet deep and in that space Nico had crammed a large antique wooden desk and desk chair, a small table placed next to the desk for his computer monitor and printer, and a folding chair on each side of the door. Any empty space was cluttered with boxes full of papers and notes, including rough drafts of lectures and research papers. The two folding chairs were piled high with books. The walls had been painted yellow, and the ceiling gray. There was no air conditioning and a small electric fan perched on top of the pile of books on the chair closest to the desk whirred softly, moving the hot air around the room. Though the room was cluttered and untidy, it was dust free and clean.

He grabbed his jacket, and with the American History exam in hand, rushed out from his office, heading for the college's media center to have copies made for his class in the morning.

Nico Guardino was well thought of at the university where, at age twenty-seven, he was the youngest tenured professor. He spent the greater part of every day at the university, often arriving by six-thirty in the morning and not leaving before seven or eight in the evening. He would use the quiet morning time to prepare for that day's lectures, and in the evening, after everyone else was gone, it was his time to relax in his office, turn the radio on low and work on the articles he wrote for the history department's weekly newsletter or do his research for his lessons.

He spent little time at his small one bedroom apartment five blocks from the campus. To him, it was only the place where he kept his clothes, slept, and showered. He almost always ate at the campus cafeteria, unless one of his colleagues invited him over for dinner. His apartment was just as cluttered as his office, with books and boxes of papers scattered everywhere. His clean clothes covered the small couch in the living room, and a small television sat on one of his end tables placed against the opposite wall. He watched little T.V., preferring to read or work on his notes and papers. He had very few dates, being totally wrapped up in his career.

That was not to say that he was not attracted to the fairer sex, and they to him. At five foot eleven and a hundred ninety pounds, with his curly black hair and blue eyes he would turn their heads when he walked by. He exuded a boyish charm, though his naivety was apparent during casual conversations. He dressed for comfort more than style, preferring jeans to slacks, and casual shirts, un-buttoned over colored t-shirts, to dress shirts and ties. The look fit him and only made him more attractive, though casual probably wasn't the proper term for his dress. "Rumpled" fit better.

He had no steady girlfriend, and hadn't for a number of years. When he did go on a date, he always seemed to steer the conversation to his job, which was the reason he rarely had a second date with the same woman. The women he dated would always stay friends with him after they stopped seeing each other, as he was handsome and charming, and seemed so innocent and naïve.

His American History class was one of the most popular classes at the university, and always had a waiting list filled with hopeful students. His passion was history and it showed in his presentations. His enthusiasm was infectious.

His lectures were liberally sprinkled with folklore. He would often start the lecture with an example of a folklore tradition and its effect on history, usually how often the course of history was guided or changed because of it. He was very well versed in American and old English folklore, and often spent hours in the library researching more to use as topics for his classes.

Nico had grown up in central California, near the foothills of the Sierra Nevada Mountains, raised by his mother. He had no brothers or sisters. His father had walked out on them shortly after he was born and his mother had had to go to work. Babysitting duties fell to his two aunts and his grandparents, and as a result he maintained close ties with his extended family. His mother would drive the hour to the city and drop Nico at her parents' place, or at school when he was old enough, then on to work. She used the time after work, during the drive home to teach him many things, using the time to his advantage. She taught him to be respectful to others, and to be honest and courteous. She still lived in the house in which he grew up, a hundred and fifty year old farmhouse she had remodeled, sitting on ten acres of land. She lived comfortably on her pension from working thirty-two years at the phone company and the interest from some very shrewd investments she made during the technology boom in the 1980's. To say she was rich was overstating her situation. A more accurate assessment was that she was very comfortable.

He would make the hour drive home to visit her every couple of weeks, and talked to her on the phone almost every day. The days he spent with her were the only times he would get a real home-cooked meal. Those days were restful and relaxing, almost like going on an R and R. He could rest and forget his cares. He felt secure and comfortable at his mother's house, spending his time reading or walking in the woods and fields on the ten acres surrounding the house. He loved the golden hills, covered with black oaks, dogwood trees and Manzanita and loved hiking them. When he left to return to the city, he felt refreshed and re-charged.

On the weekends he did not spend at his mother's he liked to go on long hikes in the hills just outside of town. He would spend hours hiking through the countryside. When the weather was not right for hiking, he would spend the day reading in his apartment or at the local Barnes and Noble bookstore. He would be so engrossed in what he was reading that he often forgot to eat until the hunger pangs intruded on his concentration.

He arrived at the media center three minutes before closing. The clerk at the front counter groaned when she saw it was him.

"Let me guess, Nico. You need something copied before I go home, right?"

"Right, Angie."

"And, of course, you need about a zillion and a half copies, which will take me at least an hour to do". She leaned her elbows on the counter and grasped her hands together in a praying position. "Geez, Nico, I gotta date tonight. Gimme a break, will ya? I've been trying to hook up with this guy for three months, and when finally he asks me out, you come waltzing in here with your cute little face and puppy-dog eyes asking for a favor." She leaned over the counter and said, "If you weren't so damn cute, I'd throw you out of here myself." She sighed, looking at him standing there with a shy smile on his face. "Alright, what is it you want?"

"You know I wouldn't ask, Angie, unless it was really important. All I need is fifty copies of this," he said, handing her the four-page exam. "Won't take long. I owe you," he said, grinning at her.

"You already owe me a half-dozen dinners, Nico. I'm still waiting to collect. All right, I'll do it, but I'm holding you to your promise. I want dinner at Martini's next Wednesday, and don't give me any of your excuses! I happen to know you are free on Wednesdays, so you better meet me there!"

"But..."

"But nothing. Be there, Nico, or else no more copies, ever!"

"OK, OK, I'll be there. Seven OK?"

"Seven's perfect. Now, how many copies did you need?"

The next morning, Nico was standing at the small desk in his classroom arranging the tests as the class filtered in. Once they all were seated, he walked around the front of the desk and said, "On my desk is your final exam. There are eight essay questions, from which you must select six you wish to answer. Each answer must be backed up by historical facts, either quotes from historical figures, dates, or events to show you know what you are talking about. I know the semester ends in two days, so before we get going, are there any questions?"

No one spoke up so Nico picked up the stack of exams and began passing them out. "Remember, your name, the date and the class number must be printed, legibly please, in the upper right corner of all pages of your blue books. Number the pages sequentially, too. You have three hours to complete it. You can begin as soon as you get the test. When you are done, place the exam on my desk, and have a nice vacation."

When he finished passing out the exams, he returned to his desk and sat down. He took one of his reference books from a drawer and opened it to the section on Cornish legends. He retrieved a pad of paper and a pencil and wrote across the top, "Giants, Mermaids, and Lost Lands: The Legends of Cornwall." Nico turned to the book and found the section he needed with the information for the talk he was preparing. He was the keynote speaker at the local history club's annual conference and he wanted to be well prepared. He had attended the conference over the last five years, and was a presenter at the last two. He was honored and thrilled that he had been asked to speak at the main banquet. He smiled to himself as he wrote on the pad, "Jack the Giant Killer" followed by "A farmer's son who lived near Land's End in the days of King Arthur." He began to make detailed notes from the book, losing all track of time and his surroundings. After a while, Nico looked up from his work and saw the entire class was busily writing their answers to the test questions. The only sounds in the room were the rustling of papers and the scratching of the student's pens and pencils as they wrote. Nico turned back to his book and continued to make notes, filling several pages in the three hours of the exam.

The beeping of his watch timer broke his concentration. Putting his pencil down, he closed the book and turned off the watch alarm. He stood up, stretched, and announced, "You have ten minutes left." He sat down again and leaned back in his chair, watching the class finish up their exams. One by one, they approached his desk and placed their exam on it. Wishing him a good summer, they left with the reminder that their exam results would be available by two p.m. the next day, and he would be happy to e-mail them their score, along with their final grade if they sent him an e-mail request.

Once all the exams had been turned in and everyone had left, Nico stood up and began gathering them and putting them in his old leather briefcase. He closed the briefcase, grabbed his jacket off the back of the chair and a folder of research notes from the desk and walked to the classroom door. Looking around once more, he sighed, knowing that another term had come and gone. He felt a bit depressed that he would not be lecturing and holding classes for the next three months, but was excited at the same time, realizing that he would have much more time to pursue his research and studies into folklore. He smiled to himself as he shut off the lights and closed the door.

Nico spent the next five hours in his office grading the exams, only stopping long enough to walk to the student cafeteria to grab a hamburger and fries for dinner. It was after ten p.m. when he finished, and he spent another half-hour entering the results on his laptop, expecting that most everyone in the class would be requesting their score and grade the next day. He yawned mightily and stretched the kinks out of his arms and legs. Locking the graded exams in his desk, he gathered his things and left his office, locking the door behind him. He walked outside, stopping at the bottom of the stairs. Raising his face to the sky he drank in the cool night air, taking several deep breaths. He turned and started walking toward the faculty parking lot where his six-year-old Volvo was parked.

As he passed the science hall, his attention was drawn to a dark figure standing in the shadows by the front door at the top of the stairs. He slowed as he passed the person, who appeared to be standing still and quiet. Uneasiness began to build in his stomach when he realized the figure was dressed all in black. Nico thought the figure had a wide flat-brimmed hat on his head and possibly had a black cape draped over his shoulders. A thin sheen of perspiration formed on his upper lip in spite of the cool night air and the uneasiness in his stomach changed to nausea. He squeezed his eyes shut and wiped the sweat from his face with his sleeve. He looked back to where the figure had been standing, but he was gone. *Am I seeing things?* He thought. He stopped walking and turned, trying to see into the deep shadows, even taking a step toward the stairs. *C'mon, Nico,* he thought, *there's nothing there.* He stood looking at the shadows for a long moment, then shook his head and walked away, the nausea quickly dissipating. He unlocked the car and climbed in. Starting the engine, he backed the car out of the parking space, put it in drive and began to slowly drive out of the parking lot. As he turned onto the street toward home, he looked one more time at the science building, seeing only shadows.

***

He watched from deep in the shadows as Nico drove away, waiting quietly for another ten minutes. He saw no one else, the campus appearing to be deserted. His attention was drawn to the sound of the door to the science building opening. As a figure stepped out he moved into his path from the darkness, blocking him. Startled, the figure stopped and gasped in surprise. Once the initial shock passed, he recognized the man blocking him and breathed a sigh of relief.

"Oh, it's you!" he exclaimed. "You startled me. What are you doing here at this time of night, and why are you dressed like that?"

"Good evening, professor. Just wanted to see how you are doing. Are you feeling well?"

"As well as can be expected, thanks for asking."

"Glad to hear that. I know your time is short, Professor, and I am here to help."

"Help? How can you help when the doctors tell me there is nothing more they can do?"

"I cannot help cure you, but I can help prepare your path to the hereafter. I would like to cleanse you of your sins before your time arrives."

"What is this nonsense you are talking about? Please, you know I don't believe in that and don't want anything to do with that stuff. So if you don't mind, I'll be on my way," the professor said as he turned away and started to walk toward the stairs.

He had only taken three steps when the twisted cloth was thrown around his neck and pulled tight. He was pulled back into the man behind him, held off-balance, and the cloth was pulled even tighter, cutting off his air. He grabbed at the cloth and struggled to pull it loose but was not strong enough. He tried to scream for help but the garrote prevented from him making any noise. The professor continued to struggle, growing weaker with each second. After less than a minute, he was almost unconscious and his struggles had nearly stopped. His assailant pulled him down to the ground, laying him gently on his back, keeping the pressure on his throat. He began mumbling what seemed to be a chant or a prayer as he took one hand off the cloth and removed a small piece of bread from his pocket. The professor's struggles had stopped and he was able to place the bread on his chest. Reaching back into his pocket, he removed two coins and placed them on the professor's eyes, then re-gripped the cloth and pulled it tighter.

He held the cloth for another three minutes, until he was sure the professor was dead, all the while reciting the prayers, finishing the recital by saying, "I give easement and rest now to thee, dear man. Come not down the lanes or in our meadows. And for thy peace, I pawn my own soul." Removing the cloth, he folded it and placed it in his coat pocket, took the bread and ate it, then removed the two coins. Holding them with the thumbs and forefingers of his hands, he raised them toward the sky, mumbling another short prayer, then placing them in his pocket. Without another look at the professor's body, he got to his feet and slowly walked away.

Chapter 2

H enderson had just finished adjusting his tie when the phone rang. He looked at his watch and saw it was just before seven a.m. *Only one reason my phone rings this early,* he thought as he reached for the phone. *Someone is dead.* He lifted the receiver off the charger and said, "Colby, what's up?"

"Hi, Lieutenant. It's Sergeant Mabry. We got a dead body."

"I figured as much. Where?"

"At the college, on campus. Campus police found it at the Science Hall while on a routine security check."

"What time was that?" he asked, as he grabbed his wallet and keys and slipped on his suit coat.

"About six-thirty this morning. They called us a few minutes ago and I sent two beat cars out there to help secure the scene. Called you next."

It was standard procedure for the campus police to enlist the aid of the city cops whenever a major crime occurred at the college. With limited personnel and resources, a major investigation was beyond their capabilities. As a result, they would turn the investigation over to the city detectives and assume a supporting role, assigning an officer to act as liaison to the investigation.

Being a relatively small college, with only three thousand students, the campus police consisted of six patrol officers, a Sergeant, one Lieutenant, and the Chief, augmented by another half-dozen unarmed non-sworn security officers. The city police were often called upon to back up the campus officers on their traffic stops or calls for service, when needed, and to assist them with any arrests they might make. Though the campus police were sworn officers, just like the city police, once they graduated from the academy their continued training was lacking and, along with the lack of experience of the officers, their ability to conduct a major investigation was almost non-existent.

Henderson Colby had been with the San Donorio Police Department for 18 years, the last twelve as a homicide detective. Located in the central valley of California and sporting a population of fifty-two thousand, the city grew up around the railroad lines and highway ninety-nine that moved the produce, cattle, and other goods up and down the length of the state. Moderate in temperature all year round, it was a good place to work and live. Summer temperatures averaged in the mid-nineties with occasional stretches over a hundred degrees. Temperatures in the winter rarely dropped below forty degrees. Being in the central valley, there were few hills and no mountains. The standing joke among the residents was that the freeway overpass was the highest point in the city. Some jokester even went so far as to attach a sign at the top that said "Vista Point".

The crime rate was low, with fewer than half a dozen homicides a year on average. When Colby was not investigating a homicide, he helped out with any robbery or serious assault investigations. The largest crime problems were the thefts of goods from the warehouses and railcars in the rail yards, and the bar fights that occurred almost every weekend when the itinerant workers would flood the local bars, their pockets bulging with their weekly pay. Hard drinking and hard fighting was often the result.

At age fifty-three, he was eight months away from retirement and was winding down his career. He groaned to himself with the news of the body at the college, hoping it would be nothing more than a natural or accidental death. He had spent thirteen years with the Los Angeles Police Department before this and had made the move to San Donorio in the hopes of escaping the crime and savagery he had had to deal with while with the LAPD.

He had been married for a short while and divorced for much longer. He liked it that way, not having to be accountable to anyone. In fact, that's what broke up his marriage so long ago. His wife did not like him being with the police department in the first place, and liked even less the "choir practices" he and his cop buddies would have after most shifts. She hated him coming home night after night stinking of booze and cigars, and constantly nagged him about it. Henderson could not understand why it bothered her so much and grew weary of what he perceived were her attempts to control what he did. The marriage soon went the way of numerous other cop marriages, ending in a messy divorce. He saw no reason to ever tread that path again. His only regret was that he hardly ever saw his daughter after the divorce. He would send birthday and Christmas cards, and call her several times a year, but never received anything from her. Their conversations over the phone were strained and short, usually ending quickly. They both felt uneasy and awkward during those calls. After twenty-five years, he still looked forward to the mail on his birthday, hoping that maybe, just maybe, she had sent him a card. For twenty-five years he had been disappointed.

"Any more information on how he died?"

"Nope. The campus police dispatcher was just told to call us to report the body and request a detective. That's you."

"Alright. Who are the uniforms at the scene?"

"Fifteen x-ray two and four, Johnson and McCabe. They arrived just before I called you. They set up a perimeter and roped it off with crime scene tape. They started a log of everyone who is there or entered the scene, and are restricting access until you get there and tell them otherwise. McCabe did say he briefly examined the body and couldn't see any obvious trauma. Apparently the corpse is one of the professors."

"Alright. I'm leaving now, so let them know I'll be there in twenty minutes."

"Twenty minutes? Jesus, Colby, you live five minutes from the campus."

"Yeah, but I haven't had my coffee yet and Starbucks is busy this time of the morning. Besides, the victim's not going anywhere."

"Damn, Lieutenant," Sergeant Mabry said, chuckling, "You're a real piece of work."

***

Nico left his apartment about the same time, walking the few blocks to the campus. As usual, he had his nose buried in a book and didn't see the yellow crime scene tape around the science building as he walked past it, and didn't notice the police cars and ambulance parked nearby.

"Professor, Professor Guardino!" a voice called out from in front of the building. Nico didn't hear it and kept on walking."

"Professor, it's me, Sarah."

Nico stopped and looked around, seeing one of the campus police officers, Sarah Ferris, running toward to him. "Hey, Sarah, what's going on?"

Officer Ferris slowed to a walk, matching Nico's strides and said, "Don't you know what happened here last night?"

"No. Something happened?"

"Yeah. There was a dead body found on campus."

Nico stopped walking and turned toward her. "What? A body? Who was it? Anyone we know?"

"The Dean of the Science Department, Professor Savage."

"What happened?"

"Don't know yet. I found him at the top of the steps of the science building this morning while making my rounds."

"How did he die?"

"Hard to tell. There were hardly any marks on the body."

"Really? Wow! Who'd have ever thought something like this would happen on our little campus!" Nico said, shaking his head side to side. Looking at his watch he said, "Look, Sarah, I've got to get to class, but come by my office later and let me know what's going on, OK?"

"OK, Professor, if I can." She turned and walked back toward the crime scene as an unmarked police car drove up.

Nico didn't move for a couple of minutes, watching the police at the science building searching the area. He noticed the officers at the scene deferred to the new arrival and he surmised, rightly, that he was a detective from the San Donorio Police Department and was in charge of the investigation. As he watched, he felt the same uneasiness from last night creep over him and a slight queasiness in his stomach. His heart started beating a bit faster as he remembered the figure he saw on the landing of the science building last night. He knew that the person he saw was not Professor Savage. The professor was only about five feet six inches tall and thin, and the figure he saw was at least six feet tall and heavier. He shook his head to dispel the feelings, took a deep breath and continued walking toward his office.

All morning Nico was distracted, finding it hard to concentrate. Since the final was over and this was the last day of classes at the campus, he started sending the students that requested it an e-mail with their test score and final grade. When he was done, he logged off his computer, leaned back in his chair, and stared out the window. A quarter hour later, there was a knock on his door.

"Hey, Nico," Sarah said, sticking her head in the office door.

"Hi Sarah. You off duty now?"

"Yeah. Just finished my shift. Thought I'd come by and visit for a bit."

Sarah Ferris had grown up just outside San Donorio on a small ten acre farm her family had owned since the late 1800's, growing mostly fruit trees. Her grandfather had bought twenty more acres in the 1930's and planted them with almond trees, not wanting to have all his eggs in one basket. Working on the farm had toned her muscles and her wiry frame fit her five foot five height. She wore her auburn hair just below her ears and her fair skin set off her green eyes. A splash of freckles across her nose added to her appearance, an appearance, coupled with her compact figure, that turned men's heads when she walked by.

She had no desire to continue the family tradition and take over the farm, along with her brother, and after she graduated high school, she moved to the city to attend college, seeking something other than the farmer's life. She worked a series of minimum wage jobs to support herself and pay for her books while her parents paid her tuition. While attending classes she became interested in the criminal justice program and changed her major to specialize in law enforcement. Once she graduated, she applied for and was accepted to the police academy, putting herself through as a student.

She joined the Campus Police Department almost a year earlier, after graduating from the academy fourth out of thirty-two cadets. Jobs in the law enforcement community were scarce, with most cities and counties cutting back on their budgets to reduce their deficits. As it happened, Sarah scored high on the written test and oral board for the campus police, finishing second. There was only one position available, but the top candidate refused their offer of employment, feeling a campus police position was beneath him. Sarah jumped at the offer, accepting the position immediately. After eight weeks of field training, she was turned loose on the campus, assigned to the graveyard shift. After half a year on nights, she was assigned to the swing shift for three months, and then went back to graveyards which she was presently working.

She loved her job and loved working for the campus police department. She planned to work there for a few years then seek a promotion. If there were no promotional opportunities, she thought she might seek a lateral transfer to the city police or the county sheriff's department.

The campus police department did not send their officers for much training, other than what was required, so Sarah often would enroll in outside training classes that interested her and would improve her skills, using vacation days to attend and paying the cost herself.

Sarah and Nico had become friends over the last few months, as Nico often worked until late in the evening, coinciding with the hours she worked. She would often stop by Nico's office to see if he was there. If he was, they would spend an hour or so talking about history and folklore, which fascinated her. She never got tired of listening to Nico's tales, and he enjoyed her company as much as he enjoyed talking about his passion. Nico considered her one of his closest friends, but Sarah felt somewhat stronger about him. She never told him of her feelings and never gave any indication through her behavior that they were anything more than friends, but she wished and dreamed that some-day there would be much more to their relationship.

"So what's going on with the death of Professor Savage?" Nico asked. He had been uneasy all morning since first finding out about the death of the professor. He couldn't stop thinking about the dark figure he had seen last night, at the top of the steps to the science building. He still wasn't sure he had seen anyone. Perhaps it had just been the product of an overly tired mind, with a bit of imagination thrown in. He had wondered whether he should tell Sarah about the figure, but then decided not to until he found out whether the professor's death was due to natural causes or not.

"Lieutenant Colby from the police department examined the body and listed the death as of suspicious origin. He found signs of trauma on the body, so we have to wait until the autopsy to find out the cause."

"When will that take place?"

"Sometime this afternoon, I guess."

"Did you get a look at the body?" Nico asked, probing for information.

She got up and went to the office door. Opening it, she looked up and down the hallway to see if anyone was there that might over-hear them talking. Closing the door, she sat back down and leaned in toward Nico. "Look, Nico, I shouldn't be telling you this stuff. It's classified and not for release to anyone but the police." She looked around again, leaned in a bit closer and said barely above a whisper, "I did get a good look at him before anyone else got there. There appeared to be bruises around his neck, and there was petechia in his eyes."

"What's that, Sarah?"

"It's broken blood vessels that occur in and around the eyes. Most often it's due to some sort of disease or sepsis, but it also occurs when someone is de-prived of oxygen, like when they are strangled or smothered."

"Does that mean he was murdered?"

"Not by itself, but it can indicate he may have died due to a lack of oxygen. There also were traces of cyanosis." Before he could ask, she continued, "I know you don't know what that is. Cyanosis is a bluish tinge to the tissues and mucus membranes that occurs when they are deprived of oxygen, and with the bruising around the throat, I'd say it's a good bet he was strangled. I would expect to see some signs of a struggle if he was strangled, but there weren't any of those marks, either. And there were no defensive marks to his hands or arms. He would have fought his assailant for his life, which would have caused some injuries. It's very odd that there were none of those signs."

"So there's no chance his death could have been by natural causes? A stroke or heart attack, maybe?"

"I seriously doubt it, though it's not totally out of the question. Maybe a sudden, massive heart attack or stroke, but something tells me there is a lot more to this than we realize. I don't know what the cause of death was, but it's pretty obvious it was a homicide."

"Will you know more later? Are they keeping you involved in the investigation?"

"I asked the Chief if I could handle the case on our end. He didn't say yes, but he didn't say no either. He said he would let me know tomorrow, but I think he will. Since I found the body, it's only logical that I stay involved."

"Will you do me a favor, Sarah?" he asked. "Will you let me know what the official cause of death is? Once you find out, I mean."

With her head tilted to one side and her brow furrowed, concern etched on her face, she asked, "Why are you so interested, Nico? Is there something I should know about?"

He forced himself to look directly in her eyes and said, "No, of course not. I'm just curious. Nothing like this has ever happened around here before."

She looked at him for a long few seconds before replying. "Well, I told you, I'm not supposed to release any information to anyone outside the P.D., but I know I can trust you, so, I'll give you a call as soon as I find out. You got to promise me you won't repeat anything I tell you."

"I promise. Thanks, Sarah. I appreciate that."

"No problem." She looked at her watch and stood up. "I better get going. I've got to be back for a meeting with Detective Colby at four and I need to get some sleep." She yawned mightily and asked, "Will you be around later this evening? I can come by your office if I find out anything new."

"Yeah, I'll be here. I've got to put together my notes for the speech next week."

"OK. See ya later, Nico.'

"Get some rest," he said as he walked her to the door, closing it behind her as she left. He walked back to his desk and sat down. He closed his eyes and placed his fingertips to his temples, trying to massage away the headache that was building behind his eyes. He made up his mind to tell Sarah about the figure he thought he saw last night. There still was a nagging uneasiness in the pit of his stomach that he didn't understand, and something dark was hiding at the corners of his memory. He kept seeing the outline of a shadowy figure, as if he was looking at it through a heavy fog at night, the edges indistinct. Try as he might, he couldn't bring it to the front of his memory, and trying only made his headache worse. "Screw it," he said to himself, opening one of his folklore books. He soon forgot about it as he immersed himself in his research. His head began to feel better and the dull throbbing behind his eyes dissipated.

Chapter 3

Jacob Sondimere was kneeling in front of the toilet bowl, leaning over it. The last couple of retches produced nothing but a small bit of thin bile that burned his throat. The nausea had lessened and he knew the vomiting was over. He wearily got to his feet and went to the sink. Turning on the cold water, he splashed handfuls on his face, washing away the sweat and cooling his feverish skin. He took a mouthful of water and swished it around his mouth, spitting it into the sink, cleansing his mouth of the foul taste that lingered after the violent vomiting. He turned off the water and grabbed the towel from the rack next to the sink. He wiped his face and hands as he walked into the small living room of the apartment. He sat on the couch, laying his head back and placing the damp towel across his forehead.

As he sat there, an overwhelming sorrow engulfed him and he began to sob softly. Large tears rolled down his cheeks and dripped onto his shirtfront. After a couple of minutes, he regained his composure and used the towel to dry his eyes. He took several deep breaths before rising and walking into the small bedroom. He stripped off the black tie and white shirt and removed his black suit trousers. His socks and underwear were next to join the heap of clothes on the floor. He padded naked to the shower in the tiny bathroom and turned the water on, adjusting the temperature until it was lukewarm. He quickly washed and then stood under the stream of water, allowing it to splash onto his face and run down his body. He stood there with his eyes closed as the water washed the nausea from him, and remembered.

He remembered how, when he was a child, his father, would not tolerate weakness in his only son, how he would beat him to toughen him up. Tears were not allowed. The punishment for crying would be long, cold hours locked naked in a small pantry with no light or food, and only water to drink. His relationship with his father was such that he could never call him "Dad". It was always "Father" or "Sir". Anything else was taken as a show of disrespect and would bring severe consequences. There was never any expression of love between them. He learned to contain his tears, his fear, and his anger, keeping it all inside until he could feel it roiling in the pit of his stomach. When it got to be too much, he would seek release by running into the woods where nobody could hear him and he could scream and scream until he was exhausted. Tears once again spilled from his eyes as he remembered, and he cried softly as the water ran over him.

When he was a child, all he knew about his father's job was what his mother told him, that his father was a "helper" to families when someone was dying. He never fully understood this, but felt it could not be a bad thing. After all, how could it be bad to help dying people and their families?

Jacob loved his mother. She always was kind to him, never abusing him or raising her voice. She would do what little she could to protect him from his father. After all, Junior, as she affectionately called him, was her only child, her baby. When she lost her battle with cancer five years ago, he took her death very hard.

He remembered being woken early by his father on his sixteenth birthday. "Get up and get dressed, son. Today you go with me, to learn what I do. Soon enough it will be your turn to replace me, as I replaced my father. Be downstairs in ten minutes, and hitch the horse to the wagon." He saw his father had hung a black suit, with a white shirt and black tie on his door, indicating he was to wear those clothes.

He clearly remembered that day. They had driven to a farmhouse twenty miles away, parking out front and walking up the steps to the porch. Before knocking his father turned to him and said, "You must always show respect to the family, to the dying, and to the house. Speak softly and clearly, though not so softly that the family cannot hear you. Do not rush things. Do whatever they ask without question. Keep your speech and actions dignified. Remember, we get referrals by word of mouth only. If you disturb the serenity of a house and the occasion, you will get few referrals and little work, understand?"

His throat felt dry and he had to swallow a couple of times before answering. "Yes, father," he finally croaked.

"Today you just watch. You say nothing and follow me. Stay close to me at all times." His father knocked on the door and stood quietly, waiting for it to be opened.

After that day, he would never be the same.

When he felt better, he shut off the water and got out of the shower. Taking one of the bath towels from the rack next to him, he dried himself then draped the towel over his shoulders and walked into the small bedroom. He felt exhausted. He stumbled to the bed and crawled under the blanket naked. He knew this feeling. The vomiting and uncontrollable shaking was getting worse and it took longer for him to recover. It wasn't so long ago that he could sleep for an hour or so after the job was done and awaken refreshed, in full control and feeling fine. Now, he would sleep for several hours and would still not feel right when he awakened. He lay on his back with his eyes tightly closed, waiting for the blissful oblivion of a totally exhausted sleep, to forget for just a while. After a short time, he drifted off.

Consciousness returned to him slowly. At first he was confused, not sure of where he was or what he was doing there, then realizing he was in bed at a cheap hotel room. He opened his eyes and saw it was dark in the room. He sat up in bed and looked at the alarm clock on the dresser. Its luminous dial told him he had been asleep for over five hours. He rubbed his hands over his face, trying to shake the grogginess he felt. After a few minutes he got up and went into the bathroom. By the time he had finished shaving, he felt much better, almost back to normal. He dressed in a clean white shirt and tied a perfect Windsor knot in his thin black tie. He brushed the dust and lint from his black suit trousers and put on his matching coat. He carefully locked the door behind him and left the building, heading to the diner around the corner.

He walked slowly down the street, keeping to the shadows as much as he could. He didn't know how but he knew he was supposed to be here, in this town, that his quest was coming to an end. He felt nervous, uneasy, and felt as if he was being watched by something so strong, so pure that his very soul was in danger. He constantly glanced over his shoulder, trying to see if he was being followed. Movements caught from the corners of his eyes caused him to throw furtive glances to the sides. Unexpected and loud noises startled him, making him jump and look around wildly.

By the time he arrived at the diner sweat was trickling down the back of his neck. He felt a deep sadness and had lost his appetite. He sat in a corner booth and ordered some food along with a cup of coffee. When the food was placed in front of him the smell and sight made him nauseous. He pushed it aside and placed his elbows on the table. Resting his head in his hands, he sat silently staring down at the table, occasionally taking sips from the mug of coffee. Forty-five minutes later he left the diner, the food untouched and the dregs of the coffee cold. He barely made it back to his apartment before the exhaustion once again overcame him. Lying on the bed fully clothed, he fell into a deep, troubled sleep.

At that time, Nico was in his office just finishing his research. He closed the book in front of him and yawned. He stood up and stretched, working the kinks out of his legs and back. As he was packing his books into his briefcase a knock came at the door.

"Nico? Are you here? Can I come in?"

"Come on in, Sarah. I was just getting ready to leave."

Opening the door, she stuck her head in and said in a stage whisper, "I've got some news, Nico."

"Really? Come, sit down and tell me about it!"

Sarah pulled the chair from the corner up to Nico's desk and sat down. "Well, I told you I went to that meeting with Detective Colby this afternoon. The whole thing was a planning session on how he wanted to work the case. He said the official word, for now, was that they didn't know if the professor's death was due to natural causes or something else."

"Did they do the autopsy yet?" Nico asked, leaning in toward her.

"It's not completed. They still have the toxicology screens to complete. They won't have that done for a few days yet."

"Did they find any injuries on his body?"

"There was bruising to the muscles of his neck, just under the skin."

"So what do they think caused the injuries?"

"They don't know yet, but Colby said they could have been from being strangled. The coroner said the bruising to the muscles looked like someone had strangled him, but wouldn't say for sure until he completed a few more tests. He is going to complete the toxicology tests in the next week or so to see if there is any trace of alcohol or drugs in the professor's system."

Nico said nothing. The feeling of uneasiness had returned and he was beginning to feel a bit queasy. He took a couple of deep breaths and started rubbing his temples again.

"Nico? You OK?" Sarah asked, rising from her chair in alarm.

Nico took another deep breath and said, "I'm fine, Sarah. Just don't feel very well. I think I'm coming down with the flu. I think I'll go home now, go to bed. I need some rest. I don't want to be rude, but would you mind?" Nico asked, motioning toward the door.

"Are you sure you're OK?" she asked again.

"I said I was fine, now please go, OK?" he said more harshly than he intended, pressing his fingers to his throbbing temples.

"Oh, OK," she said, taking the hint. "I'll go now. Got the duty anyway. I've got another meeting with Detective Colby tomorrow morning. You go home, Nico, get some rest." Sarah got up from the chair and walked to the door. Opening it, she left without another word.

Damn, Nico thought. *That was a dumb thing to do. Now I've hurt her feelings.* Sarah was the only person besides his mother he felt comfortable confiding in. He hoped he had not damaged their relationship, as the time they spent together talking was one of his favorite pastimes. He suddenly realized that her friendship was very important to him, and the last thing he wanted to do was to hurt her feelings, to make her feel bad. He wished he had not been so short with her.

***

Henderson Colby sat in his recliner at his apartment, going over his notes from the crime scene, a glass with four fingers of Jack Daniels in it on the end table next to him. He knew without a doubt that the professor had been strangled and from the marks on his throat whoever killed him possessed extraordinary strength. He knew it also indicated the murderer was very angry at the time, otherwise there wouldn't have been so much bruising. He was willing to bet that the autopsy would reveal a crushed trachea and a broken hyoid bone. He was anxious to get the report, which, he had been told, would be ready in the morning.

What puzzled him was the breadcrumbs on the body and ground around it. The crumbs had been found by the crime scene technician and collected on Colby's orders. He wasn't sure of the significance of the crumbs, or that they were even connected to the crime, but if there was one thing he had learned it was that everything at a crime scene had the potential to be the case-breaking piece of evidence.

What really was odd was the fact he was unable to find any crumbs under the victim. How could there be crumbs on and around a prone body, no crumbs under it, and no other remnants? Did the killer bring the bread with him? Was he eating at the time of the murder? Was it the victim who had eaten the bread, and if so, what happened to the rest of it? Colby didn't yet have the answer to the questions running through his mind. He recorded them in his notebook to make sure he would come back to them later and to remind him to have the professor's stomach contents analyzed.

He sighed and rubbed his eyes. Reaching over to the glass, he took a drink, feeling the liquor warm his throat as it made its way to his stomach. He settled back in the chair and closed his eyes, letting the warmth from the alcohol spread through him. The murder again crept into his mind. He sat up and picked up his notebook and began reading again, occasionally making more notes. When he was done reading he started at the beginning again, looking for something he may have missed, something significant, something that seemed out of place.

He read and re-read his notes for the next hour, sometimes adding a short notation, other times erasing things. It was just past midnight when he finally put the notebook down. He sat up in the chair and rubbed his eyes. He yawned mightily, then picked up his glass and drained the watered down liquor, the ice having melted, then stood up and stretched. He turned off the lights and headed to the bedroom.

Chapter 4

As Colby headed off to bed, Jacob Sondimere was just starting his shift at the hospital. He had been employed as the night janitor for the last three months. He liked working the night shift as there were few people around and they left him alone. They would say hello when he passed by, but his quiet manner, dour look, and curt replies were a barrier to further conversation. He made no friends, and the nurses, technicians, and doctors on the night shift paid him little attention. As such, he pretty much had free rein around the hospital, going anywhere he chose.

He pushed his dust broom along the hallway in front of the nurse's station and down the hallway. He knew they had just made their rounds, checking on the patients and giving them their medications, and they would not be wandering around the hallways for at least another hour. He noticed the three nurses were sitting in a group with the on-duty doctor, drinking coffee and talking quietly. He continued down the hallway at his normal leisurely pace, sweeping as he went, turning the corner. Near the end of the next corridor he arrived at the records room. He leaned the broom against the wall and quietly unlocked the door with the copy of the key he had taken from the spare key cabinet during his first week of work. The theft had gone unnoticed and he had been able to have a copy made and replace the original without anyone being the wiser. He grabbed his broom and stepped into the room, closed the door and re-locked it behind him, then made his way to the furthest computer terminal. He knew he was safe, as no one ever looked for him on these quiet night shifts, assuming he was sweeping and cleaning up somewhere in the building. He never left any indication he had been where he wasn't supposed to be, or that he was doing anything else other than his work.

He snapped on the small desk lamp in the cubicle and booted up the computer, typed in the password he had found written on the desk under the keyboard, and accessed the records of the most recent patients. He spent the next fifteen minutes looking through the records until he found the perfect one. Smiling to himself, he shut down the computer, retrieved his broom and left the room, locking the door behind him.

***

At half past eight that morning, Henderson walked into the coroner's office and helped himself to a cup of coffee from the coffee maker on the file cabinet.

"Hello, Henderson," Doctor Beauchamp said, watching him help himself to one of the bagels from a plate next to the coffee pot. "How about some coffee? Maybe a bagel?"

Taking a bite of the bagel, Henderson replied, "Thanks, Doc, don't mind if I do." He made his way to the chair opposite the desk and sat down. Taking a sip of the coffee he said, "Not bad coffee, Doc. You make this?"

"As a matter of fact, I did. Glad you're enjoying it. The bagel, too."

"Yeah, great bagel. Thanks."

"You're welcome. Now, I imagine you want to know about the autopsy on the professor?"

"Yep. Are you all done?"

"Yes, it's done. You were right, Henderson, he was strangled. The larynx was crushed and the hyoid bone broken, plus the obvious signs of bruising, the petechia in his eyes, and the cyanosis. I've got your copy here," Doctor Beauchamp said, handing him a sheaf of papers in a red cover. "Oh, yeah, I checked the stomach contents liked you asked and there was no bread. And I found something during the autopsy that might interest you," he said, as he got up, walked over to the coffee pot and poured himself a cup. He added a teaspoon of sugar and a packet of dairy creamer, stirring it as he walked back to his chair.

Henderson thumbed through the autopsy report and when Dr. Beauchamp sat across from him he asked, "What's that, Doc?"

"I found a recent surgery scar on his abdomen. It apparently was from an exploratory procedure a month or so ago. He was riddled with cancer."

"What?" Henderson said, slopping coffee from his cup onto the floor as he leaned forward toward the desk.

"He had a moderate sized tumor in his large intestine, and it had metastasized to some of his other organs."

"Really?" Henderson asked, setting his coffee cup and half bagel on the desk.

"His liver, pancreas and one kidney all had tumors. I imagine he must have been in quite a bit of pain. I would think he would have been under a doctor's care, or least receiving some sort of pain medication. The blood work will tell us what when it's completed."

"How sick was he, Doc?"

"I would say it was terminal. With the amount of cancer I found, I don't think there was much medical science could to for him."

"Geez, that's horrible. How long do you think he would have lived?"

"Maybe six months, nine if he was lucky."

"That little time, huh? Wow, I can't imagine having to deal with something like that! Poor guy."

"It's all in the report, Henderson. You can read it for yourself." Standing up, Doctor Beauchamp looked at his watch and said, "I've got a lot of work to do and not much time to do it, so why don't you go back to your office, read the report, and call me if you have any questions."

"Yeah, sure Doc." Henderson got up and walked slowly toward the door. He opened it then turned back toward the doctor. He walked back to the desk and picked up the half-eaten bagel. "Thanks, Doc. I'll call you later," he said as he left. As he walked down the hallway he opened the folder and began reading the report.

An hour later he was sitting at the conference table at the police department updating the administration and other investigators on the case. Directly to his left was the Chief of Police. Continuing around the table was the who's who of the Police Department. In descending rank was Captain Anders, the Investigations Bureau Commander, and two other detectives. Next to the detectives was the Campus Police Chief, and next to him was Officer Sarah Ferris, who had been designated as the campus police contact on the case. As such, the campus Chief had flexed Sarah's hours so she worked dayshift and would be available to assist Henderson and the other detectives in the investigation. Henderson had just filled them in on the preliminary results of the autopsy, including the professor's health situation.

"So, according to the medical examiner, he only had six to nine months to live. Now, I don't know if that has anything at all to do with the murder, but it's something we need to consider," he finished.

The Chief interrupted him, asking, "Do we have anyone looking into this?"

Henderson gritted his teeth, thinking, *you fucking idiot! Didn't I just say I got the results an hour ago?* He took a breath before answering, calming himself. Keeping his expression neutral, he answered, "Not yet, Sir. That's why I asked Williams and Toranski to be here. I will be briefing them further after we are done and will have them start checking around."

Henderson had little respect for the Chief, who had been selected by the city council and city manager ten months earlier from a group of candidates for the position when the former chief retired.

The Chief came from a moderately sized northern California police department with fifteen years police experience, where he held the rank of Lieutenant. His background check revealed that he had spent less than two years as a patrol officer before being promoted to Sergeant and being assigned to the administrative division. Five years later he was promoted to Lieutenant, taking over as the services division commander. Eight years later, he applied for and was selected as the Chief of the San Donorio Police Department. Henderson resented the fact that the Chief had very little patrol experience and street time, had spent most of his time in administration hidden away in his office, and he didn't trust the Chief's judgment because of this lack of experience.

Since taking over as Chief, few changes of any consequence had been instituted in the department. After taking over, the Chief had taken the time to talk to every employee on a one-to-one basis to find out what changes they wanted, what they liked or didn't like, and what concerned them most about the department. He then met with the department as a whole and outlined what his vision was for the future of the department, what he had learned from the employees, and what changes he planned to make in the next few months. That was seven months ago and he had to yet make the policy and equipment changes he promised. Once he was done with the interviews and department meeting, he literally disappeared into his second story office and was rarely seen by the rank and file members. He was not highly thought of in the department, to say the least. Henderson, and many others felt the new Chief showed little leadership ability and questioned his dedication to his new department.

"Henderson, I want you to give this investigation the highest priority. I want this thing solved without delay! We cannot have a murderer running around our fair city, terrorizing our citizens who are depending on us for protection."

Careful, Colby, Henderson thought. *Just say what he wants to hear and let it go at that!* "I agree, Sir. We'll get this guy and our citizens will feel safe again!" *God, what drivel. I feel like I'm part of a bad soap opera!*

"That's the spirit! Now, let's get out there and get to work!" the Chief said as he stood up.

"Sir," Henderson said as the Chief turned away and started for the conference room door, "The press is waiting in the lobby for a statement. You want me to handle it for you?" *Please, God, make him say no.*

"That's OK, Henderson, I'll take care of it," the Chief replied, smiling at him.

"Fine, Sir. Well, I've got work to do." Henderson got up from his chair and said, "Officer Ferris, would you come with me, please?" then turned and walked out of the room.

Sarah was taken by surprise by his request and was a bit flustered. She recovered quickly, got up and hurried after him, dropping some of the papers she was carrying along the way. She stooped down and retrieved the fallen briefing sheets from the floor, then once again quickly walked after the Lieutenant who by this time was at the end of the hallway rounding the corner. His voice drifted back to her, "Are you coming, Officer?"

"Right behind you, Lieutenant," she said as she ran after him.

***

Nico arrived at his office at nine a.m. to continue his research for the talk he was to give in a few days. He hung up his jacket and placed his briefcase on his desk, then made the short walk to the student cafeteria and bought a latte and a cranberry muffin and made his way back to the office. Closing the door, he walked to the small window and stood looking out to the campus, thinking of the shadowy figure he saw the night of the murder. He couldn't get the image out of his mind and the more he thought about him, the more he knew it wasn't the first time he had seen him. The now familiar queasiness was back. He just couldn't remember where he had seen the figure, but he knew it was not a good memory, not something he wanted to remember. He sighed, shook his head and turned back to his desk. Opening his books, he immersed himself in his research, driving the uneasy thoughts from his mind.

Two hours later he heard a soft knock on his door. "Professor? Are you there?"

"Come in Sarah." Nico quickly ran his fingers through his hair, somewhat smoothing the rumpled mass as she opened the door and entered. "What's up?" he asked, smiling at her, as he scraped the remnants of his muffin and the now empty coffee cup into the trash basket next to the desk.

"Just came from a meeting with Lieutenant Colby at the police department. He had some new information on the case."

"Oh yeah? Anything significant?"

"Not really. He got the autopsy results today. Professor Savage was strangled to death, as we thought, but the autopsy also revealed he was very sick."

"What was wrong with him?'

"He had an advanced case of cancer. The doctor thought he only had a few months to live."

"Really? Poor guy. Is it connected to the murder in any way?"

"Detective Colby doesn't know, but he's not discounting it. I've been checking around the campus and it doesn't seem like anyone here knew of his disease. He doesn't have any family around here, and only a couple of close friends. He kept his illness a secret."

"He must have been under a doctor's care, though, right?"

"I would think so. I'm supposed to meet Lieutenant Colby at the police department in a half hour or so. We're going to try to access Professor Savage's records. He apparently had some surgery a month ago that nobody knew about."

"He had to miss some classes if he had surgery. Is there any record of him being gone recently?"

"I checked and found he had applied to attend a conference in San Diego five weeks ago. The conference was supposed to last a week, but the professor took the next week off on vacation. His request form stated he wanted to spend an extra week to do the tourist bit there. He was gone two work weeks."

"With his regular days off, that was fourteen days. Plenty of time to have the surgery and recover enough so no one would know when he came back to work."

"That's what I thought. Look, Nico, I've got to report in to the Lieutenant. I'm supposed to be getting myself some coffee and he expects me back soon. What are you doing later?"

"Nothing planned. I'm gonna stay here for a while longer, but I'll be done around two or so. Why?"

"Well, I thought maybe we could grab a bite of dinner this evening. I mean, if you're not busy and, you know, you want to. What do you say?"

"I say sure, Sarah. I'd like that."

Sarah felt a warmth spreading inside her, and knew her face was turning red. "OK, great. Want me to pick you up here, or you want to meet somewhere?"

"How about if I meet you at the restaurant? That will give us both time to finish up what we have to do and get cleaned up. Does Dino's Ristorante on Oak sound ok?"

"Sounds great. I love Italian food. Ok, I'll meet you there at six?"

"Six it is, Sarah."

She smiled, a sudden shyness enveloping her. "Fine. See you there." She left the office closing the door behind her. She walked down the hallway with a bounce in her step, smiling ear to ear.

Sarah drove back to the police department and met Lieutenant Colby upstairs in the investigations conference room. "Hello, Sir. What do you need me to do?"

"Hi, Sarah. I need you to run down the professor's movements during the two weeks he was off. Call the hotel in San Diego and talk to the security director. Find out if the professor was there the whole time. I want to find out where he had that surgery and who did it. You may not be able to get that info because of the doctor-patient confidentiality, but explain to them you are investigating the professor's murder and he has no immediate next of kin. Maybe they will give you what you ask for. You can use that desk over there," he said, pointing to a small desk in the corner. "Any questions?"

"No, Sir."

"Good." Colby placed his hand on her shoulder and, lowering his voice, said, "I hope you understand how much I appreciate your help, Sarah. I don't want you to think that you are being given busy work or unimportant stuff, because it's not. Everything, and I mean everything, we do on this investigation is important. If there is one thing I've learned, it's that sometimes the most innocent appearing, unimportant snippet of information may be the one that breaks the case."

"Lieutenant Colby," Sarah replied, taking his hand in hers, "I don't think that. You and I both know that I have no experience in investigations. I'm just grateful for the opportunity to work with you on this case." She smiled at him and said, "I'm going to get to work now. I'll let you know as soon as I find anything out."

Smiling back at her, Colby said, "Thanks, Sarah." After a moment's pause, he asked, "Say, would you like to grab a bite to eat tonight, after we are done for the day?"

Sarah was surprised at the question, and after a brief moment, said, "Thanks for the offer, Sir, but I've got plans already."

"OK, no sweat. And, please, call me Henderson." He smiled at her and walked back to his office, closing the door after him. Sarah sat at the desk, turned on the computer and began making some calls.

Chapter 5

Nico dialed his mother's number, this being his regular day to call her. She picked up after three rings, and as always, sounded delighted to hear from him.

"Hi, honey," she said, "I was hoping you would call today."

"C'mon, Ma, you know I call you every Wednesday. How are you?"

"I'm fine, son. How are you?" She paused a moment then asked, "Everything alright? You sound troubled."

"I'm OK, Ma."

"No, you're not, Nico. I know when something's not right, and something's not right with you. Tell me what it is."

"It's nothing, Ma, really."

"C'mon, honey, tell me"

"It's really nothing. I just haven't felt right the last few days. There was a murder on campus a couple of days ago and something about it has bothered me."

"What is it that's bothering you, Nico?"

Nico took a deep breath, the memory of the figure he saw intruding on his mind. He let it out slowly then said, "I saw something that night and I can't get this uneasiness out of my mind." Nico took another calming breath, then told her the whole story. "So as I was walking past the science building on the way to my car, I saw what appeared to be a figure dressed all in black standing on the landing. I stopped and stared, and the more I looked, the more uneasy I felt. I felt queasy, started shaking and began to perspire. I looked away for a moment, and when I looked back the figure was gone. The next morning I found out Professor Savage had been murdered on that very landing that night."

"Oh my God! That's horrible! Did you tell anyone about it?"

"I'm sorry to say I didn't."

"Why not, honey?"

"Ma, I'm not even sure I saw someone. It was so dark, and I was so distracted, had a lot on my mind, that I don't know if I really did see that person. Maybe it was just the shadows."

"Even so, Nico, you need to tell someone, the police or whoever is investigating it. This isn't something that you should keep to yourself."

"But what if I'm wrong, Ma? I don't want to cause any problems."

"Don't worry about it, Nico. If it turns out to be nothing, so be it. At least you will have the peace of mind that there was no one there."

"That's true."

"On the other hand, if there was someone there, it could very well have been the killer and what you saw may help the police capture him. So you see, this is a win-win situation. Tell someone, honey, someone you trust. You will feel better."

"I suppose so, Ma. OK, I will." Nico sighed. "How do you always know the right thing to say, Ma?"

"I'm your mother, Nico, that's how. Besides, you already knew what you had to do before you called me, didn't you?"

"You're amazing, you know that?"

"Yes I do, and I love you. You go do what you have to, Nico, OK?"

"OK, Ma. I love you."

"I love you too, baby. Call me later and let me know how it went."

"I will. Bye."

Nico hung up and leaned back in his chair, deep in thought. He tried to picture that night and what he saw, trying to see through the shadows on the science building landing, trying to get a better picture of the figure. He gave up after a few minutes and instead thought about how he would tell Sarah what he had seen. There was no question in his mind about whom he would tell. Sarah was the only one he really trusted to take him seriously. Besides, they had a dinner date and he knew the case would come up during their conversation. It would be the perfect segue to what he wanted to tell her.

***

Sarah had spent most of the morning on the phone, making several long distance calls to San Diego trying to track the professor's movements. She eventually contacted the conference coordinator and was able to confirm that Professor Savage had paid his conference fees and registered the afternoon before the conference started. She also found that he had signed up to attend several of the seminars, but that no one could say for certain whether he had actually attended them. The coordinator said that there was no attendance record kept for the individual seminars, so they had no way to tell if the professor was there. Sarah asked for and got the attendee list and called several of them to try to confirm Professor Savage was there, but no one could say for sure they saw him. Since there were over a hundred and fifty attendees, she realized how easy it would be for someone to remain anonymous.

She called the hotel where the conference was being held and where the attendees were staying and found that the professor had made a reservation for only two days, rather than the five the conference was scheduled for. The hotel confirmed he had checked out after the second day. Sarah suspected the professor had gone from the conference to a hospital to have the surgery, but which one did the procedure? Was it their local hospital in San Donorio, one in San Diego, or somewhere else? Sarah thought she should start with Professor Savage's personal physician, Doctor Roberts, and looked up his number in the professor's personnel file. If anyone had the information she needed, he would.

Sarah thought about what Lieutenant Colby had said about the information being private and confidential. She doubted Doctor Roberts would readily give her the info, but she thought she could get around it if she made him think she already had it and her call was to merely confirm what she already knew. She quickly formulated a plan and dialed the doctor's number. When he answered, she introduced herself and told him she was assisting with the investigation into the murder of Professor Savage.

"I know there is a doctor-patient confidentiality issue here, Doctor, but I think we can avoid any ethical or legal problems. Professor Savage is deceased and can't give his permission to release his records, and there is no next of kin on record. Yes, I realize that in such cases a court order is needed, but I really don't want to see his files. All I need is for you to confirm the information I already have. Are you willing to do that? Thank you, Doctor, you're cooperation is greatly appreciated. No, I'm sorry, I can't tell you where we are in the case. It's an active investigation, and we are pursuing several leads, but other than that, I can't be more specific.

"Now, I know Professor Savage went to San Diego a few weeks ago, supposedly to attend a conference. The autopsy revealed that he had had a surgical procedure about the same time as the conference, an exploratory that found he was riddled with cancer. In fact, the medical examiner said he was terminally ill. Is that correct? It is? Good.

"I've been able to trace his movements in San Diego and found out that he didn't attend the conference. In fact, he checked into the hospital and had the surgery done. I'm assuming the results were sent to you, weren't they? OK, were they sent to your office in town or the hospital here? The hospital, eh? OK. Who sent you the results? Was it the surgeon or did they come from the hospital, uh, what was its name? Oh yeah, Regional Medical Center downtown. That's right, it says it right here in my notes. My file says the surgery was performed by a, hold on, it's a very poor copy, hard to read. It looks like it might be a Doctor Anderson. Really? It was Doctor Miller? Wow, it looked like Anderson to me!

"Listen, Doc, the medical examiner estimated the professor only had a few months left to live. Is that true? Oh, gosh, that poor man! Is that information in his records at the hospital? Yes, I would assume it was, but I had to ask. Just needed to confirm it. Thanks very much Doctor. You help is greatly appreciated. No, that's all I need for now. If I need anything else, I'll call back. Goodbye."

Sarah hung up the phone and completed writing her notes, then leaned back in her chair and smiled. She was pleased at how she had convinced the doctor to cooperate and that she had so easily gotten the information. Looking at her watch she saw it was getting close to three o'clock. She looked around and saw the office was nearly empty. Lieutenant Colby was in his office on the phone. She walked to his door and knocked. He waved her in and pointed to the chair opposite his desk. Sarah sat and waited until he had completed the call.

"What's up, Officer Ferris?" Colby said, leaning back in his chair.

"I ran down the professor's movements in San Diego."

"Good. What did you find out?"

Sarah told him of her calls to San Diego and the professor's doctor. "That pretty much confirms what we suspected, Sir."

"Yep. Thanks, Sarah. Good work. One question, though. You said his doctor told you the results of the operation were sent to him at the hospital?"

"That's right. Is it important?"

"I don't know yet. It could be. Do you know anyone at the hospital?"

"Yeah. One of my best friends from college works there as a licensed vocational nurse. Why?"

"I need you to call and confirm those records are there. Also, find out about their record system, like who has access to the patient records and how access is gained, the usual background stuff."

"Okay, Lieutenant. If it's all right, I would like to leave after that, unless you have something else for me?"

"No, that will do it for today, Sarah. Just make sure you complete your report tomorrow morning. I'll need it by ten, okay?"

"Fine. Thanks, Sir," Sarah said as she stood to leave the office. "I'll get right on it."

Sarah went back to her desk and called the hospital, asking for her friend. Once she came on the line, Sarah asked her about the records system and how it could be accessed. She told Sarah that all she knows is that the records room was on the fourth floor. She said she never had reason to access any of the patient's files so she wasn't familiar with the system. She told Sarah she would forward her call to an administrator friend of hers.

After a couple of minutes on hold, the phone was answered by a Mrs. Gabriel. Sarah introduced herself and explained why she was calling. Mrs. Gabriel, told her that all their records were computerized and that access was strictly limited.

"How is access controlled?" Sarah asked. "Is it limited to certain people and how easy is it to get into the records room or use the computers at the nurse's stations?"

"Well, to get into the records room when it is open one must have the proper credentials, along with a key. It is kept locked even during normal business hours. If someone wants to check a patients' records, they have to fill out a request sheet and give it to one of the techs. They have to have a reason to access the records."

"So they can't just go there and get whatever information they want?"

"Absolutely not!" Mrs. Gabriel replied. "Patient confidentiality is a serious matter here."

"What about accessing the information at the nurses' stations?"

"One would have to log on to the records system, and it's password protected. The computer logs the name of the person who is logging on, and what files they accessed. Each person authorized to access records has their own password, so it's easy to keep track of them."

"What about after business hours? Is the records room alarmed?"

"No, but we have staff on duty twenty-four hours a day on that floor, so they would know if any unauthorized persons tried to get in there. They would have to go directly past the fourth floor nurses' station to get to the records room."

"What about employee access? Can anyone put in a request for the records?"

"No. As I said, that information is strictly controlled. There are only certain people who can request a patient's records, like the doctors, supervising nurses, and, of course, the administrators. And their request is reviewed by the records supervisor before approval can be given."

"It seems like you have everything tightly under control," Sarah replied. "I think that's all I need for now. Thanks so much for your cooperation. If there are any other questions, can I give you a call?"

"Of course, Officer Ferris, any time!"

"Great! Thanks again, Mrs. Gabriel. Bye."

Sarah hung up the phone and spent the next half-hour compiling her notes. When she was done, she looked at her watch and saw it was just past four p.m. She left the office and headed home to get ready for her dinner date with Nico.

Chapter 6

S arah drove into the restaurant lot and parked near the front door. She looked in the rear view mirror, checking her face and hair. While getting ready earlier, she put her makeup on, then removed it because she thought it was too much, then re-applied it, then removed some until she was satisfied with how she looked. She put her hair up, then took it down, then put it back up. Eventually she decided to brush it back down. Now she surveyed herself in the mirror on the car visor and wasn't happy with her appearance. She was very nervous about meeting Nico, and dabbed the thin sheen of perspiration from her upper lip and forehead. She rested her head against the steering wheel, almost starting to cry. She was not happy with the way she looked and what she was wearing, and was afraid this date would be a disaster. She didn't know whether Nico thought of her as just a friend, or if she was just an acquaintance. It was beyond hope that he could feel more than friendship for her. She thought about just driving home and skipping the date, but then realized she couldn't do that to him, that she cared too much for him to stand him up like that.

She took a couple of deep breaths to compose herself, then went into the restaurant. Nico spotted her as soon as she came in and stood up, waving at her. She smiled and made her way to the table.

"Hey, Sarah." Nico said. "Gosh, you look great!"

Sarah felt the blood rush to her face and she looked down, embarrassed by his compliment. "Thanks, Nico. You look pretty good, too."

Nico came around the table and pulled her chair out for her, then returned to his seat. "Really, Sarah, you look very nice. I'm so used to seeing you in your uniform, it's nice to see what you really look like off duty."

Sarah was secretly pleased at this. She had wanted to ask him out but never could get up the courage. She always thought he could never be interested in her, that she wasn't his type. "Thanks, Nico."

"I ordered some wine, a nice Chianti, if that's ok?"

"Sounds good." She looked around, then leaned in toward him. Lowering her voice as if she was afraid someone was listening, she said, "I've got a lot to tell you. This case is really getting interesting"

"Let's order first, OK?" Nico said, as their server approached. Nico ordered the gnocchi with marinara sauce and sausage while Sarah ordered the veal parmigiana. He poured them both a glass of wine and raised his glass. "A toast. Here's to a quick resolution of your case."

"Amen," Sarah replied. They both took a drink, then sat silently for a minute, each at a loss for words. Sarah broke the silence, saying, "I told you Professor Savage was terminally ill with cancer."

"Wait, Sarah. Let's not talk about that right now. Why don't you tell me about yourself. Did you grow up here in San Donorio?"

They spent the next two hours over dinner and wine, then dessert, talking softly about themselves and their future plans. Nico told her about growing up in the old farmhouse and how much he liked it there. He told her it was the only place he really felt at peace, where he could forget his worries and obligations.

They were so lost in each other they didn't hear or see anyone else in the restaurant. Nico suggested they go back to his apartment for more coffee and Sarah readily agreed. Neither one of them wanted the evening to end.

Once back at his apartment, Nico put on a pot of coffee and sat next to her on the couch. Sarah's heart was racing and she could hardly look at him, hoping he would finally make a move on her. Instead, he asked about the case, saying, "Tell me everything you know about the case, OK? When you're done, I have something to tell you."

Sarah was a bit disappointed, but started talking about her day. She told him all about the investigation and what they had learned of the murder and the victim. "The problem with the information is that it offers no clues as to who killed him, or even why he was murdered."

"There's just not enough information yet, Sarah," Nico replied. "I'm sure as time goes on, you'll turn up enough to solve it."

"I hope so. Tomorrow, we're going to interview any family we can find, and his closest associates at the college. Maybe they can shed some light on the professor's life. He was a pretty private guy, but someone must know something that could be of value. I figure the more we learn about the professor, the closer we will get to solving this.

Changing the subject, Nico asked, "How do you like working on your first homicide?"

"Pretty interesting, and very exciting. I'm learning a lot about investigative procedures, too."

Nico chuckled quietly. She was like a kid in a candy store when talking about the investigation. He found he couldn't stop staring at her.

"Nico? Hey, Nico, did you hear me?"

"What? Oh, I'm sorry. I lost my train of thought for a moment. What were you saying?"

"I said that unless we come up with something quickly, the chances of solving this become less and less. Every training class I've had, and every book I've read says the first forty-eight hours in a homicide investigation are the most important."

Nico got up and poured them both some coffee. He sat on the couch and took a sip from his cup. Looking at Sarah, he took a deep breath and said, "Sarah, there's something I need to tell you."

"What is it, Nico?"

"That night the professor was killed I left my office about a quarter past ten. I was walking to the parking lot and as I passed the science building, I got an uneasy feeling as if someone was watching me. When I looked around, I thought I saw someone standing in the shadows on the landing."

"Really?" Sarah said, leaning toward him, her interest piqued. "That would be within the time frame the coroner gave us for the murder. Can you describe the person?"

"Not really. I'm not even sure I saw anyone. It made me uneasy and I looked away for a few seconds. When I looked back, the figure was gone."

"Did it appear to be a man, or a woman?"

"It seemed to be a man, but like I said, I can't be sure there was anyone there. It could just have been a trick of the poor lighting and the shadows."

"Try to think, Nico. This may be important. Any other impressions you got?"

"Well," Nico replied, looking down at his hands clasped in his lap, "It seemed to be a man, just because of his size. He appeared to be fairly tall, maybe six feet or more. If there was someone there, he was dressed all in black."

"Did you get a look at a face?"

"No, it was too dark, too many shadows. Sarah, I can't be sure there was anyone there, but I got this very weird feeling there was, and I was being watched. It was so strong that I started feeling a bit nauseous. I had to look away for a short time. The shadow was no longer there when I looked back. It was very strange. I just thought you should know."

"It could be important, Nico. Anything could be important. It's too bad you didn't see more. I'll have to include this in my report, Nico, and Lieutenant Henderson may want to talk with you."

"Yeah, I figured that. Can I ask a favor?"

"Sure, anything Nico."

"Any chance you could leave that out of the report?"

"I don't know, Nico. I think it needs to be in there."

"It's just that I can't be sure if I really saw anyone. I think it was just my being tired, along with a trick of the lighting. Give me a couple of days to think about it, to be sure that I wasn't just seeing things."

Sarah thought for a moment then said. "OK. You get two days, then I've got to let the Lieutenant know."

"Thanks Sarah."

Sarah looked at her watch. "Oh my! It's after midnight! I better get going. I have to be on duty by seven in the morning."

She stood up and said, "I had a great time, Nico. Thanks for the dinner and conversation."

Nico stood up, too, facing her. He took her hand in his saying, "I had a good time, too. We'll have to do this again, if you want to."

"That would be fun. I would love to."

Nico smiled at her and walked her to the door. Opening it, he turned toward her. "Goodnight, Sarah. Come by the office and see me tomorrow, OK?"

"OK," she replied. She wished he would take her in his arms and kiss her, but she knew how shy he was, so she did the next best thing. She suddenly leaned in, standing on her tip-toes, and kissed him on the mouth, then walked out of the apartment.

Chapter 7

Nico arrived at his office just after eight the next morning. He was prepared to spend the day straightening up his papers from the last term and cleaning up the clutter in his office. He wanted to do some more work on his keynote address for the conference, but had to find the right reference books first, which were most likely buried under one of the mounds of books and papers scattered on his desk, filing cabinets and spare chair.

Three hours later he had made some progress. At least he had found the reference books he needed, had gotten rid of a bunch of old class notes and student papers that went unclaimed from two semesters ago, and he had gone through a couple boxes full of pamphlets and books that he no longer needed. He sat in his chair for a few moments of rest, leaned back and closed his eyes, relaxing and listening to the music on his radio.

He was still thinking about his date with Sarah the previous night. He had come to the realization that there was much more to her than he assumed. She was smart, motivated, and very attractive. Their time together had been so enjoyable that he had found himself looking at his watch every so often, wondering what she was doing and when she would visit him.

When he went to bed last night, he had difficulty sleeping. Not because of her, but because he kept thinking of the dark shadow with the black cloak. He had an uneasy feeling he had seen him before but couldn't quite wrap his mind around when or where, or under what circumstances. All he knew was that it was an unpleasant experience.

There was a soft knock on his door, then it opened and Sarah stuck her head in. "You busy, Nico?"

Nico sat up and smiled at her. "Not at the moment. Come in, Sarah."

Sarah walked in and looked around, saying, "Wow, the office looks so much bigger now!" She sat in the chair next to his desk. "I want to thank you again, Nico, for last night. I had a great time."

"Me, too. So, what's going on? Anything new on the case?"

"Not yet. Lieutenant Colby and I have been trying to run down the professor's family and friends. He's looking for the family and I'm making my rounds through the campus trying to find anyone who was close to him."

"Any luck?"

"Not yet. Everyone I talked to, the other professors and staffers, know him or know of him, but so far there's no one that could be considered a close friend."

"I hardly knew him myself. Just to say hello to when we passed or were in a meeting."

Sarah looked at her watch and stood up, saying, "Geez, I gotta get going. I've got a meeting at the police department in a half hour and there's still a couple of people I need to contact before then. I'll call you later, OK?" Looking at her watch again, she headed for the door.

"Sure, Sarah. I'll talk to you later," he said to her back as she left the office, disappointed that she couldn't stay longer.

Sarah sat in the meeting with Lieutenant Colby, the Chief, and the other investigators, half listening to a synopsis of the investigation up to that point. She still had not found anyone who knew about the professor's private life. She was at a dead end as far as any possible leads through the campus personnel. From what she was hearing, Colby had not found any close relatives either.

"The best I could do is to check with the hospital and see who they had listed as his next of kin," he was saying. "They were kind enough to provide me with that information. The only family he has is a sister in Iowa, and a few cousins scattered around the States. I did manage to contact her, and she said she hadn't seen him in more than twenty years, and hadn't spoken to him for at least five. She couldn't tell me much about him and didn't know of anyone out here that I could contact." He looked around the room and said, "Unless anyone else has more info, this investigation is going nowhere fast."

The Chief shook his head; "Not good enough, people. There has to be something more to this guy. Do your best to find out what it is, understood?"

Sarah felt small and insignificant, sitting there with all the others, but her determination was not blunted. She just knew there had to be more, that they were not going in the right direction. She felt it was just a matter of time before someone found the one piece of information that would re-charge their investigation.

The meeting continued after the Chief left, with Sarah telling them the results of her contacts at the college. Henderson suggested they continue looking for the friends and family, but if there were no concrete results by the end of the day they would try something new tomorrow. The meeting broke up and everyone headed to their desks to make some more calls. As Sarah got up to leave, Detective Colby stopped her. "I'm going to the medical examiner's office in a bit. He's completed the professor's autopsy and has some information for us. Want to go?"

Sarah jumped at the chance. She had never been to the coroner's office before or seen an autopsy, or even talked to the M.E., and was looking forward to the experience. Besides, she wanted to hear what the examiner had to say about the autopsy results.

Two hours later Sarah and Detective Colby were walking out of the Coroner's office, talking about what they had found out from the Medical Examiner.

"It surprised me," Detective Colby stated, "That there was that amount of morphine in his system. I didn't know he was that sick."

"The M.E. said he was terminal. Gave him a few months to live. How could he keep that from everyone?"

"That's just it. He couldn't have kept it from everyone. Someone had to know. Someone at the hospital, for sure, had to know."

"I agree. I'm wondering why wouldn't they come forward with that information?"

"They probably thought it wasn't important to the investigation, and they do have to honor the doctor-patient confidentiality." Henderson stopped walking, thinking for a moment. He turned to Sarah and asked, "Would you call the hospital and find out which doctor prescribed the morphine?"

"Sure, Lieutenant. I'll do it as soon as I get to my desk."

"Thanks, Sarah. You've really been a big help with the investigation, you know, and I really appreciate your efforts."

Sarah felt the blood rising to her cheeks. "Thank you, Sir. It's been nice working with you and the others."

"That's great. Let me know what you find out about the doctor. I've got to get some of the evidence we collected to the County Crime Lab, so we'll get together later this afternoon when I get back and you can fill me in."

A half hour later Sarah hung up the phone and collected her notes. She had just talked with the hospital and had the name of the doctor that had been treating Professor Savage and who had prescribed the morphine. She asked to talk to him, but was told he had the night duty that evening and wouldn't be in until ten p.m. She decided she would go see him that night and find out what he had to say. He must know the name of someone who was close to the professor, or who the professor had listed as his next of kin. She could only hope he would give her that information. She walked over to Lieutenant Colby's office, but saw he was not in. She asked the clerk if she knew when he would be back and was told he would not be coming in until the morning. He had gone to the county jail on a tip from one of the Sheriff's Investigators to interview a person that might have some involvement with their case.

"Did he say what that was all about?"

"No, just that it was a long shot, but he wanted to make sure he covered all the bases."

Sarah went back to her desk and sat down, thinking she would call Nico and see if he wanted to go with her, just to keep her company. She picked up the phone and called and they agreed to meet at a local coffee shop at nine for a latte while she filled him in on the investigation, then drive to the hospital to interview the doctor.

Nico was glad she had called him, not only because he wanted to see her again, but also he didn't want her to go alone. He knew he was being a bit overprotective, but he worried about her being in such a potentially dangerous profession. He also knew that he was being silly and she would be very upset with him if she ever figured out his motivations. After all, she was the one with the training to handle any dangerous situations, not him, and he wondered how much help he really would be in an emergency.

He finished up at the office by six that evening, locked up and went to his apartment to grab a quick bite and shower before meeting Sarah.

Sarah arrived at the coffee shop a few minutes early and saw that Nico was already there, sitting at a table near the back of the room. She had worn her uniform for the interview, thinking that it would lend a more professional and serious air to the doctor, and couldn't help but notice the looks she got from the other customers as she made her way to the table.

"Hi, Nico. Been waiting long?"

Nico stood up and said, "No, not long. Just got here a few minutes ago. Can I get you something?"

"Just a latte."

"OK. Be right back."

Nico returned with their drinks and sat down. "Anything new on the case?"

"Not much. Lieutenant Colby went to interview some guy at the county jail, but I don't know what his connection is to the case."

"Is he a suspect?" Nico asked.

"I don't know. The investigations clerk told me only that Henderson had gotten a call from the Sheriff's Office about him and felt he needed to talk to him to make sure he has no connection to the case. I do wish I knew why they felt they he needed to be interviewed though."

"I guess it's best to be as thorough as possible," Nico mused. Looking at his watch he said, "Think we should go?"

"Yeah. It'll take us a few minutes to get there, but we may still be a few minutes early. That actually may be good. We can talk to the doctor before he starts his shift. It may mean less interruptions."

"Good idea. You driving?"

"Yes. I've got a department car out front," Sarah said as she got up and put on her police jacket.

Fifteen minutes later they were at the nurse's station on the hospital's fourth floor, waiting for the doctor. The duty nurse was the same one Sarah had talked to over the phone.

"Anything else occur to you since the last time we talked?" Sarah asked.

"No, Officer. I've been thinking about it but there's nothing else I can think of." Looking past Sarah, she exclaimed, "Here comes the doctor now."

Sarah and Nico turned around and saw Doctor James Martin walking toward them, a smile on his face. He appeared to be in his early fifties, with graying hair. He was slim and over six feet tall. He carried himself with a dignified air. Extending his hand to Sarah as he approached he said "Officer." He turned to Nico and asked, "Professor Guardino? My daughter speaks very highly of you."

"Really? Does she work at the college?"

"Actually, she's been a student in several of your classes. She's enjoyed them quite a bit. You must be good at what you do if she liked them. She's not one to take her studies seriously," he mused, smiling at them. He turned to Sarah asking, "So, what can I do for you, Officer Ferris?"

"We've been having difficulty finding a next of kin for Professor Savage. We haven't been able to locate any family he's had recent contact with, and there doesn't appear to be anyone at the college he was close to. I know that a patient's records are privileged, but we need to find someone who can act as next of kin so we can take care of some administrative needs, and who may be able to provide some information regarding the professor's life."

"Like what, Officer?"

"Well, we're trying to track his movements the last couple of months to see if anything occurred that may cause someone to murder him. So far, his past is a blank."

"So what specifically can I do?"

"I would like to know who the professor listed as his contact on his medical forms. Since you are, or were, his primary doctor, you could get that info for us from his records."

"Hmm, I'm not sure I can, Officer, as much as I would like to. It's not that I can't get the information, I'm just not sure I can legally release it."

Sarah had known that would be his answer and had thought long on how she would handle it. She needed to try to convince him to get her the name in spite of his reluctance to do so.

"I understand your concerns, Doctor, but I'm not asking for anything regarding his treatment or any of the diagnoses, just a name. It's really important that we find someone that knows him intimately. They just might have the one piece of information we need to help solve the case. Whoever did this needs to pay for his death. He can't be allowed to escape justice, Doctor, and it's just one little piece of information, just a name."

"It's that important, Officer?"

"Yes, Sir, it is. Look," Sarah said, lowering her voice, "If it is against your policy, which we're not sure it is in the first place, it's such a minor intrusion. Besides, we don't reveal our sources. There would be no record of this in my report."

"I don't know, Officer. You are very convincing." He thought a few moments then replied, "Tell you what, let me look something up in my office. I'll be back with you in just a few minutes. Wait here." Doctor Martin walked off and Sarah turned to Nico.

"Doesn't look too good, Sarah," Nico uttered.

"Let's wait and see, Nico. Maybe he'll find something that tells him he can give us the information."

They walked over to a couple of chairs and sat down to wait. As Nico waited, lost in his own thoughts, an uneasy feeling started to come over him. He started to feel like the room was closing in on him. He felt uncomfortable and his heart was beating faster. He was starting to perspire and it was getting difficult to catch his breath. It was like there was something bad in the air, permeating the room, some kind of evil virus or disease, and he was breathing it in with every breath. Nico looked around the room, scrutinizing each face, not sure of what he was looking for. No one seemed to be the cause of his feelings as far as he could tell, and there was no one else in the room or the adjacent hallways, just a janitor pushing his cart down the dimly lit hallway. He took a couple of deep breaths and shook his head, trying to dispel the mist in his mind.

Forty feet away, Jacob Sondimere pushed his cart slowly along the hallway. He had seen Nico and Sarah talking with the nurses and Doctor Martin when he got off the elevator. It bothered him that the police were here, talking to the doctor. He guessed rightly it had something to do with the death of the professor, but he didn't know exactly what. He worried that it was about him, that they knew about his visits to the professor when he was here recovering from an earlier surgery. He wondered if they had made a connection between him and the professor. He knew it would be difficult for them as no one knew of the visits. They always took place late at night, just before Jacob was to get off work. Still, it was unnerving.

He had met the professor by chance. Jacob had gone to one of the empty rooms to clean it, unaware Professor Savage had been moved into it earlier that evening. He apologized profusely and started to back out when the professor asked him to stay for a moment. Not knowing why, Jacob stayed, introducing himself. He felt he was compelled to stay, that he was meant to meet this man. They talked for a half hour before Jacob excused himself, saying he had to finish his chores. As he left the room, he knew he had to find out more about this man, why he was there and the seriousness of his illness. The next evening he took the spare key for the records room and in the morning had a copy made, replacing it the first chance he had when he went to work that night. Late into his shift, when things quieted down and the nurses were finished with their rounds, he snuck into the records room and looked up the professor in the system, finding he was terminally ill. Doctor Martin had estimated he had less than three months to live. Jacob knew at that moment why fate had brought them together. It was God's way of telling him his particular skills were needed again.

He looked back at the officers as he walked down the hall, glaring at them, directing his dislike and worry in their direction. He rounded the corner, heading toward his assigned cleaning area.

"Nico? Nico, are you OK?"

Sarah's voice snapped him out of his funk. "Yeah, I'm OK. Just got a bit of a headache." He took a couple of deep breaths and closed his eyes for a moment.

"Hey, Nico, here comes the doctor." Sarah stood and walked toward the nurses' station. Nico quickly stood and caught up with her.

"Officer Ferris," Doctor Martin said. "I've reviewed our policy and the law and I'm sorry to say I can't help you. It's clear that giving you the information you asked for would violate our patient-doctor confidentiality, even though the patient is now deceased. Good luck with your investigation. If you will excuse me, I must start my rounds now." He shook hands with Sarah and walked off.

Sarah and Nico headed for the elevator, walking in silence. Sarah seemed to be absorbed in her own thoughts so Nico waited until they were in the elevator on their way down before speaking.

"Sorry, Sarah. Wish it could have gone better for you," he said, placing his hand on her shoulder."

Sarah looked at him, smiling from ear to ear. "That's OK, Nico," she said, holding up a small piece of paper, slipped to her by the doctor during their handshake. "I think this is what we we're looking for."

Chapter 8

S arah waited until they were back in the car to open the slip of paper. Neatly printed inside was a woman's name and address.

"This address is just one block from the professor's apartment," Sarah exclaimed. Turning to Nico she asked, "Do you know a Donna Lapin, Nico?"

"Never heard of her. Why?"

"I was just wondering if she was one of the staff at the college, maybe another instructor?"

"If she is, I don't think our paths have ever crossed."

Sarah looked at her watch, frowning. "It's near eleven. Too late to call her or go see her tonight. I wonder what her relationship was with Professor Savage. Was she just a friend, or maybe a girlfriend?" Looking at Nico she said, "I'll have to do it tomorrow."

Nico smiled at her; "I can see how it's just driving you nuts that you can't contact her tonight. How about if we meet at my office in the morning and see what we can find out?

"I would like that," Sarah answered, starting the car.

The next morning, Nico had breakfast at the college cafeteria. He was hoping to see Sarah there, but she didn't show up. A few minutes before they were to meet he started walking to his office. On the way he stopped off at the human resources office and asked if Donna Lapin worked for the college. He found out she didn't and was even more curious about her relationship with the professor. When he arrived at the office he saw Sarah walking quickly toward him.

"Hi Sarah," he said, waving at her. "Got some news for you."

"I've got big news, too. Let's go in," she said, indicating his office.

Nico turned to unlock his door, saying, "I checked on Donna Lapin at HR and guess what I found out?"

"She's not an employee at the college."

"Damn, how'd you know that?"

"I got here a bit early and checked with HR."

"And here I was thinking I'd saved you some time and actually was being a help in the case!" Nico said, grinning at her.

"Well, it's my job to think of stuff like that." Placing her hand on his arm she continued, "But it was really sweet of you to do that. Thanks."

"Did you call her?"

"No. I'd rather hit her up cold than give her a chance to think about it before I get there. Might prevent her from hedging on the truth a bit."

"You think she might lie to you?"

"I've got no reason to believe she would, but it's a 'just in case' scenario. I've found it makes for a better interview if I catch them off-guard."

"You are really devious, Officer Ferris."

"All part of being an ace crime fighter, Nico."

"Look, I'm not busy this morning. Can I go with you?"

"Ah, I don't know. I'm really not supposed to have you with me, but I'd like the company and it's just an interview. Pretty harmless stuff."

"I can take that as a yes, then?"

She thought for a couple of moments, then smiled and answered, "OK, Nico. Shall we go?"

It took Sarah fifteen minutes to drive to Lapin's house. As she pulled up in front in her campus police car, a woman standing on the porch turned, and seeing the police car, hurried off the porch toward them. Sarah and Nico were not yet fully out of the car when the woman began talking.

"Thank God you're here," she said, walking up to Sarah. "I can't get her to answer the door and I'm very worried."

"Slow down, Ma'am. What's your name?"

"I'm Irene. I live across the street. Donna was supposed to meet me twenty minutes ago for our usual walk."

"Are you talking about Donna Lapin? Is this her house?" Sarah asked, pointing at the porch the lady had been on when they arrived.

"Yes, Donna Lapin's house. I don't know what to do. She never misses our walking dates."

"When was the last time you talked with her?"

"Yesterday afternoon. She called me and confirmed we were to meet in front of her house at nine a.m. When she didn't show, I started to get worried."

"What did you do then?"

"Why, I knocked on the door and rang the bell. After about five minutes or so I went home and tried calling her on the phone. It just rang and rang."

"Did you check with any of the other neighbors? Maybe she had to leave for some reason."

"No. I didn't, but she's not close with anyone in the neighborhood but me. If there was an emergency and she had to leave, she would have contacted me. She doesn't drive, you see, so I would have been the one she asked for a ride."

"OK. Wait here, please. We're going to try knocking on the door. If that doesn't work, we'll try calling her again. If I need to, I can call her with my cell phone." Turning to Nico she said, "C'mon, Nico, let's go check it out."

Sarah and Nico walked to the front door and Sarah rang the doorbell a few times. They could hear the chimes ringing inside the house. After a few minutes without getting a response, Sarah got the phone number from Irene and tried calling. After twenty rings, she disconnected the call. She walked to the front windows and tried looking in, but the drapes were pulled closed. Turning to Irene she asked, "Does Ms. Lapin usually keep her front drapes closed?"

"Not usually during the day. Sometimes she doesn't open them until around lunchtime, though."

"Ok. I would like you to go back to your house and call the police. Tell them Officer Ferris is requesting a beat unit to help in a welfare check. Will you do that for me?"

"Ok, Officer."

Once she left, Sarah turned to Nico. "I don't like this, Nico. Something's not right. I'm going to try the front door, see if it's locked. You stay here and wait for the other officers."

Nico just nodded and started to walk to the sidewalk as Sarah went up to the front door. She tried the knob and found it was locked. She rang the doorbell again, calling out to Lapin. Still receiving no answer, she left the porch and started to walk down the driveway next to the house. She tried the side door and finding it unlocked, went into the garage.

Nico saw her enter the garage and started after her, not wanting her to go into the house alone. Her discomfort with the situation had alarmed him and he felt she may need help, though he wasn't sure what he could do. As he entered the garage, he saw her standing by an open door leading to the house, her weapon drawn and pointing at the floor. Startled by the noise he made coming in, she turned toward him, starting to raise her weapon. She immediately saw it was him and lowered her gun.

"Nico! What are you doing? I could have shot you!"

"Sorry, Sarah, but I thought you might need some help."

"I asked you to stay out front. Go back out there and wait for the officers."

"I can't. I'd be too worried about you."

"Nico, this is what I do. It's my job, and I'm trained for this. You aren't. Now, please, go back out front!"

"I can't. I'm going with you."

"I haven't got the time to argue with you, Nico. Are you going to do what I asked or not?"

"Not, Sarah, so you might as well quit wasting time."

She sighed and shook her head. "Alright, Nico, but you stay behind me, understand?"

"Yes, Officer," he replied, grinning at her.

She turned back to the open door, shaking her head. Nico couldn't see the smile on her face as she slowly entered the house, calling out "Police! Is anyone home? Ms. Lapin?"

Nico followed her into the house, staying directly behind her as she moved slowly through, checking each room. Nico marveled at her thoroughness during the search. He saw how she entered each room, leading with her pistol, quickly turning the corner and crouching down, sweeping the room with her gun. His heart was pumping and the adrenalin was coursing through his veins and he thought if he had this strong of a reaction, what must she be feeling? He was amazed that she seemed to be so calm and controlled under such stressful conditions, not knowing what awaited her in each room she entered.

She had checked the living room, kitchen and sitting room without finding Lapin, and started down the short hallway that lead to two bedrooms and a bathroom.

As they moved slowly down the hallway, Nico started to feel the same uneasiness he had experienced at the hospital the previous night. He sensed an evil presence had been there. He felt the queasiness come over him and began to perspire. His vision began to blur and he found it hard to breathe. He leaned against the wall for a moment, trying to catch his breath, and reached out to touch Sarah on the shoulder.

Sarah turned at his touch and saw Nico leaning up against the wall. The look on his face and his sweaty, pallid appearance alarmed her. "Are you alright, Nico?" she whispered over her shoulder.

"I don't know. I'm not feeling very well. You go on, Sarah. I'm going to wait here for a minute, catch my breath."

"OK. Stay here, I'll be back in a couple of minutes."

As Sarah moved slowly down the hallway Nico sat on the floor, breathing deeply. Sarah came out of the bedroom after a couple of minutes and moved further down the hallway, quickly checking the bathroom and last bedroom. She walked back to Nico and crouched next to him, putting her hand on his shoulder. "Feel any better, Nico?"

"A little. I guess you didn't find Miss Lapin?"

"Actually, I did. She's in the first bedroom. She's dead, Nico. I think she was murdered."

"Oh my God. How was she killed?"

"Strangled, just like the professor."

"That's terrible. When do you think it happened?"

"I would say sometime last night. I checked the body and there is a bit of rigor mortis, and the post mortem lividity is really pronounced, so I would say she was killed six or seven hours ago." Sarah stood up and said, "Are you alright here? I've got to go call the department and report this."

"Yeah, I'll be fine, Sarah. Go make your call."

She walked off to the living room and once she was out of sight, Nico got to his feet and took a deep breath. He had an urge to see Lapin's body, though he couldn't put his finger on why. He just knew he had to see her. He moved quickly down the hall as quietly as he could, thankful that the floor was carpeted. He went into the bed room and saw Lapin on the bed, lying on her back in her night clothes, eyes closed and arms at her sides. The covers had been pulled down to her waist and Nico assumed Sarah had done that while checking the body. He walked over to the bed and gazed down at her. She looked like she was sleeping peacefully. There were no obvious marks on her body, though he could see some slight discoloration on her neck, partially covered by the high neckline of her nightgown. He noticed there appeared to be some sort of crumbs on her chest and the sheets next to her body.

He stood there for a few moments, staring at her, and once again he started having difficulty breathing. His vision began to blur and he again felt dizzy. Suddenly, he had a flash of a man in a black suit with a black hat standing over Lapin, muttering softly as if he were praying. Startled by the sudden image, he took two staggering steps backward, reaching out to find something to steady himself. He could not tear his eyes from the body.

"Nico! What are you doing here?" Sarah asked, coming up behind him. "This is a crime scene. You shouldn't be in here, contaminating things!"

Sarah grabbed him by the arm and gently pulled him back toward the doorway. The physical contact with her snapped him out of his mood and he turned to her. Taking a couple of deep breaths, he half-smiled. "Sorry. I just wanted to see the body."

"Why, Nico?" she asked.

"I don't know, Sarah. I just know it was important. If it makes it any better, I didn't touch anything."

"Well, that's good. The police are on their way. Let's go wait for them on the porch."

They made their way to the porch where Sarah had Nico sit in one of the chairs by the door. Nico took out his handkerchief and wiped the perspiration from his face. He sat there with his hands clasped on his lap and his head down.

"You don't look so good, Nico. You're sweating and are as pale as a ghost. What's going on?"

He looked up at her, forced a smile and muttered, "Just a bad reaction to seeing the body, I guess. I'm not used to dead bodies." Changing the subject, he asked, "Do you think her murder is connected to the professor's?"

"I'm certain it is. It's too much of a coincidence to think it isn't. What are the odds that the only person who was close to Professor Savage ends up being the next murder victim?"

"Yeah, you're probably right. I was thinking the same thing. So, who else could have known about Donna Lapin?"

"Well, Doctor Martin, obviously. Probably the charge nurse we talked to. I'm sure she would have access to the records, some of the administrators, maybe even some of the floor nurses. There could be quite a few, when you think about it."

"True, but isn't it odd that she was murdered the same night you contacted the doctor for her name? Somebody had to overhear you, or was told about your inquiry."

"But who, Nico? There were only three or four nurses on duty last night."

"I don't know, Sarah. It's got me stumped."

Sarah heard a car drive up and turned to the street. "Hey, here comes the police," Sarah said. She started down the porch steps to contact them and fill them in on what she found, angry that she wouldn't be able to find out what Lapin's connection was to the Professor.

Chapter 9

Jacob couldn't sleep. He was exhausted from having been up all night and longed for some rest, but was too upset over what he had done to sleep. The regret he felt was churning inside him, even though he knew it was necessary to kill the woman. She was the only one who knew he had visited Professor Savage, the only one who could connect them. Her death was necessary, but the blame was not his. It belonged to the woman cop who was asking all those questions at the hospital last night and the man with her.

He hated that she had to die, and the tears started flowing, burning down his cheeks as he lay in his bed. He wept for her, for her death, for having been forced to do something he didn't want to do. He drew some small comfort that he had performed the ritual properly, easing her passing.

He suddenly felt sick to his stomach and barely made it to the bathroom, vomiting into the toilet. He continued to retch for several minutes after his stomach was empty. When he felt better, he rinsed his mouth out with water, splashed some on his face and returned to his bed, laying down and closing his eyes. He didn't feel safe yet. The cop was asking too many questions at the hospital and wherever he went, he felt eyes watching him. It would only be a matter of time until someone might remember him visiting the professor. Though he was very careful in making sure no one at the hospital knew, he couldn't be certain his secret was safe.

He knew he had changed the way he conducted his business, but no one called for his services any more. His was a dead occupation, yet he knew it was his calling from God to continue assisting people with their path to heaven. It was a service he had been providing all his adult life, a useful service, even though people no longer believed in it. It was still his duty, his destiny to continue to smooth their path.

He felt the weight from the sins he had taken on dragging him down. Sometimes he felt he couldn't continue, that he had taken on too much. He worried for his own soul. Who would take his sins from him when it was his time to leave this life? It was a concern that troubled him more than he would admit.

Though he was frustrated and depressed, he knew he would continue his service. This wasn't the first time he had felt this way, and he knew that when he performed another service, assisted another poor soul, he would again believe in the importance of his work. It had happened seven times before in the last two years, three in Fresno, twice in Modesto, once in Hanford, and once in Stockton. Each time, he had watched the local papers to see if there was any news of the deaths and was pleased to see that only one listed the death as "suspicious". It figured that a smaller town like Hanford, with a population of less than 50,000 and a police department of forty-five would take a closer look at the death. Their homicide rate was most likely just a few a year and their investigators would not be burdened with a large open case load as in the larger cities. He had used a pillow to smother that client, and though listed as suspicious, there had been no witnesses nor any evidence to prove it was anything other than a normal death due to a terminal illness.

When the article appeared in the paper, on page two, he packed his meager belongings and left, heading south to San Donorio. None of the other six deaths were listed anywhere other than in the obituary section and he assumed they were written off as caused by their illness.

He didn't feel bad about these deaths, even though it wasn't time for the client to depart. They were dying and would succumb soon. He just hastened their transition by a couple of weeks, a month at most.

After more than a year without anyone calling for his service, he had sold his small home and set off, looking for other work to keep him in money while searching, with no luck, for clients in need of his special talent.

He was living in Stockton working as a driver for a package delivery company when the first opportunity came his way by chance. While delivering a package, he found the recipient to be a severely ill man, living alone, suffering from the effects of a lifetime of smoking. Breathing with the aid of an oxygen tank, the emphysema having destroyed his lungs, he could barely walk across the room without having difficulty breathing. Jacob paid him a late night visit a few days later.

Of the three in Fresno, one was a patient at an assisted living center Alzheimer's wing, another was at his home assisted by a hospice center as the cancer spread its way through his body, and the third suffered from kidney failure. In those instances, the opportunity to assist them happened during the course of his employment with a medical supply company as a delivery driver. He got lucky with one client in Modesto. He was staying at a cheap hotel in one of the more seedy parts of town and while eating at a nearby greasy spoon café he overheard two women talking about an elderly woman, an invalid, who lived in the building next to his and was slowly wasting away due to her advanced age. They opined that she would not last more than a couple of weeks and one even said she would be glad when she died, as she was tired of having to go there every day to clean and feed her.

He learned that once the old lady was fed dinner and put to bed, the caretaker would go home. He waited two days, watching the building to make sure the client was really alone all night. Once he knew for sure she was alone, he completed his service, helping her transition on the third night.

As Jacob lay on his back, drifting toward sleep, he thought he would have to find out what the cop had learned from Doctor Martin, and who was the man with her? Why did he make him feel so uneasy? He would have to find out more about him and the cop. She may be a danger to him, a danger that might have to be eliminated.

***

The next morning, Sarah was at the regular morning meeting of the investigators, recapping the investigation into the Professor's murder, and what little info they had in the death of Donna Lapin. Sarah told them she thought it was important to interview all the people that were on duty at the hospital two nights ago. "We need to find out who knew about Lapin being listed as his next of kin, and who told whom about it."

"And that will help us how?" one of the detectives asked.

"If we can identify everyone who knew about her, we may have a list of possible suspects. All we need to do from there is find out who had a motive and opportunity to murder her."

"Good idea, Sarah. Would you like to handle that?" Detective Colby asked, smiling at her.

"Yes, Sir, I would," she answered.

"Then the assignment is yours. When do you think you can interview them?"

"I'll try to get to them today, but maybe not until later this afternoon. They all work the night shift, so they're probably sleeping during the day."

"Okay. Let me know right away if you turn up anything."

"Of course, Sir."

Turning to the rest of the group he asked, "Has anyone checked to see if there have been any other similar homicides around the state?"

"I'm doing that, Lieutenant," one of the other detectives said. "So far, no luck. I've searched for unexplained and unexpected deaths and have gotten a bunch of hits. I'm working my way through them, but it's a slow process."

"Alright. Keep at it. If there is nothing else, let's get to work," Colby said, indicating the meeting was at an end. The detectives picked up their papers and coffee cups and left the room. Just as Sarah was about to leave, Colby said, "Sarah, stick around for a minute, please."

Sarah sat back down, waiting until the room cleared. Once everyone was gone, Detective Colby sat next to her, looked at her for a moment, and said, "I don't know what your relationship is with Professor Guardino, but I do know that he was with you when you went to interview the hospital staff the other night, and he accompanied you to Lapin's house yesterday. From this moment on, he is not to be with you while you are conducting your investigation, understood?"

"Yes, Lieutenant."

Colby softened his voice. "Listen, Sarah, you're doing an excellent job. You've been a real asset to us. Just keep up the good work, but remember we can't have civilians involved in an active investigation, especially a murder investigation. You may be putting him in a dangerous situation, Okay?"

"Okay, Sir. Sorry, I didn't think it would do any harm."

"So far it hasn't, and I want to keep it that way. So, now that we've resolved that little matter, how about you get going on those interviews?"

"Right away, Sir," Sarah stood up, grateful that Colby had been so low key in handling the situation with Nico. She made her way to her desk and called the hospital, asking for the HR department. She was given the names of the hospital employees she needed to contact, but was told they wouldn't provide her with their home phone numbers.

Sarah wasn't too concerned about that, as she figured she could find most of them through directory assistance or through the white pages of the local phone book. After she completed her call to the hospital, she called Nico's cell.

"Hey Nico, got a minute?"

"Sure, Sarah. What's going on?"

"I kind of got my ass chewed this morning at our staff meeting. Detective Colby told me I'm not supposed to be taking you with me on this investigation."

"Well. That doesn't surprise me. I always thought we were pushing it a bit. Did you get in much trouble?"

"Not really. Colby was nice about it. Kept it just between the two of us, but I got the feeling that was my one and only warning."

"Sorry, Sarah. I'm partly responsible for that, you know."

"Not really, Nico. I shouldn't have let you tag along. So, no more, okay? I'll be doing things on my own from now on."

"Alright. Will you still keep me informed of what's going on?"

"Sure. I gotta get going, Nico. Want to meet after work, maybe grab a bite to eat?"

"I'd love to, Sarah, but I'm going home today, going to stay the night at my mother's house. I'll be back tomorrow around noon, so I'll call you then. Maybe we could meet tomorrow?"

"Sure. I'll call you if anything breaks. You be careful driving. I'll see you tomorrow."

An hour later, Nico left the campus and walked the short distance to his apartment, unaware that he was being followed.

Chapter 10

Nico was driving the back roads to his mother's, foregoing the major highway that would get him there in an hour for the winding country road that allowed him to enjoy the scenery he loved so much. Winding through the gold colored fields and green forests of the foothills served to calm him, giving him a serenity he hadn't felt in quite a while. He drove leisurely, passing through the small towns nestled at the Sierra foothills, taking his time. He didn't know there was a stolen pickup truck a quarter mile behind him, just far enough behind to not be constantly in Nico's rear view mirror.

Jacob had stolen the truck last night after he followed Nico and had found out where he lived He parked it at dawn just down the street from his apartment. He had no idea what he was going to do. He just planned to watch Nico for a couple of days, find out more about him before he figured out what action he needed to take. He felt Nico was dangerous to him though he didn't know why he felt that way.

He had found out who the female cop and her companion were after talking with the nurses at the hospital. It worried him that they were trying to find out more about the professor's life and his friends and family. He thanked his lucky stars that he had the foresight to eliminate the problem of Donna Lapin. If they had found out about her, she could have provided a link to him and he couldn't have that. Now, more problems were arising because of them. He needed something to distract them, some sort of diversion. He saw how they interacted and realized theirs was more than a purely professional relationship. Perhaps the best way to distract the lady cop was to deal with the professor. He would see.

Following Nico along the winding road, seeing him driving along without a care in the world, he made up his mind. He knew what he needed to do. He saw Nico turn up the driveway to a farm house, and drove on past it. After a half mile he made a u-turn and headed back toward the city.

Sarah spent that day and the next morning calling the hospital staff, interviewing them over the phone, if they agreed to it. If they balked at the phone interview, she set up meetings with them to do a face-to-face. If they didn't answer or their machine picked up, she left a message asking for a return call. Of the seven employees on the list, two agreed to a phone interview and two others wanted to meet. She was unable to locate a phone number for one and did not receive a return call from the other two so decided to go to the hospital later that night to contact them.

Neither of the two she was able to talk to on the phone could offer any new information about the professor's family or friends, though one of the nurse's aides told her that one night a few weeks ago she had walked past the professor's room and thought she heard men's voices inside. At the time she assumed it was from the television in the room, but when she went to check on him an hour later, she found him alone and noticed there was no T.V. there. Sarah was excited about this small bit of information as she now knew there was someone else recently in the professor's life, someone who may be able to shed some new information on the investigation. The next morning she called the hospital to find out if the other staff members on her list were working that evening and to let the administrators know she would be conducting the interviews that night. Hanging up the phone, she leaned back in her chair, smiling to herself, pleased with the progress she had made. She knew the new information was sketchy, but with each tiny bit she received the solution to the murder was getting closer. She spent the next hour and a half catching up on her reports, then decided to walk across the street for a latte and a few minutes to herself.

Sarah walked to Lieutenant Colby's office and gave him her reports, asking if he wanted to get some coffee with her. He refused, saying he had another meeting to attend with the chief. She told him she would be back in twenty minutes and left the office.

As she walked out the front doors of the police department she looked at her watch, thinking that Nico should be back from his mother's soon. She was hoping he would have called her by now and wondered why she hadn't heard from him. Shrugging it off to his leaving his mother's house late, she pushed the pedestrian control button and waited for the light to change, pulling her cell phone from her pocket.

When the traffic signal changed she stepped off the curb and started across the street, concentrating on dialing Nico's cell. She had taken four or five steps into the crosswalk with the phone to her ear, listening to it ringing on the other end and did not hear the racing engine of the truck speeding toward her. At the last moment, she looked to her left and saw the pickup bearing down on her. She froze in shock briefly, long enough for her to realize she would not be able to avoid the speeding truck. She took a step backwards as the truck bore down on her, almost appearing to be aiming for her, and braced herself for the impact when she was yanked violently backwards so forcefully that her feet flew up. The truck sped by, barely missing her. She hit the ground hard on her back, banging her head on the pavement. She saw a flurry of exploding lights, then everything faded to black as she lost consciousness.

She could hear voices talking, though it sounded as if they were far away. She couldn't quite understand what they were saying, but she sensed that the person talking was concerned about something. She concentrated on the voices, catching a word now and then, listening carefully as they gradually got louder and clearer. After a minute she was able to understand most of the conversation

"Her blood pressure is fine, and her other vitals seem to be ok, but I'm worried that she hasn't regained consciousness yet. It's been over an hour and that concerns me."

"Is there a concussion?"

"Probably a slight one. At least there was no skull fracture, no thanks to you."

"Didn't have much of a choice, Doc. That truck would have done a lot more damage than the bump to her head."

"I know. Sorry about that. It's just that I'm concerned about her."

"I am too, Doc. How long will she have to stay here?"

"Hard to say. At least overnight, but maybe longer. Depends on the tests once she regains consciousness."

"I want to go home today," Sarah said.

The doctor and Lieutenant Colby turned toward her and saw she was awake.

"Well," the doctor said, "Welcome back. How are you feeling?"

"Like I got run over by a truck," Sarah said, shading her eyes with her hand.

"You almost did," he said, "Except for the quick work of Lieutenant Colby."

"Really? What happened?"

Henderson stepped to the side of the bed and said, "A minute or so after you left my meeting was cancelled, so I decided to catch up to you and take you up on your coffee offer. As I came out of the office, I saw you waiting at the curb and hurried toward you, but the light changed when I was still a few feet away. You were distracted, I think by your phone, and you started across the street. I heard a pickup coming toward you and it seemed to be accelerating. I knew the driver wouldn't be able to stop in time, so I ran up and was just able to yank you back by your coat."

"Wow, Henderson, you just might have saved my life," Sarah said, sliding up in the bed to a sitting position and holding out her arms for a hug. Henderson leaned in and gently hugged her, afraid he might hurt her.

"Sorry about the bump on the head," he said, "but I didn't have time to be too gentle."

"Don't worry about it. I'd be in a lot worse shape if you weren't there."

"Look, Sarah, I'm not sure about this, but it didn't seem to me it was just a coincidence that the driver of the pickup wasn't stopping for the light."

Sarah looked at him, speechless for a moment. "What do you mean?"

"When you started across the street, the truck was a ways back from the intersection, going fairly slow. As you walked off the curb, that's when I heard it accelerate. It was coming at you quickly, and the driver was looking right at you."

"So what are you saying?" Sarah asked.

"Just that it looked like he was aiming for you. I'm sorry, Sarah, maybe I'm wrong. I don't want to worry you, but that's the impression I got. What really concerns me is if my impression is right, why would he want to hurt you?"

"Beats me, but it's got to be connected to the case. Maybe I've gotten a bit too close, or learned something that threatens him. The only problem is I have no idea what it is."

He took her hand and smiled. "Don't worry about it. You just rest and when you get back to the office, we'll go over everything and see if we can figure it out together. I'm going to assign an officer to watch over you tonight, just to be safe."

Sarah laid back down, pressing her hands to her temples. The pain in her head was throbbing, making her eyes water.

Seeing this, the doctor told Henderson, "Let's leave her alone now. She needs her rest." Turning to Sarah, he firmly admonished her, "I'm going to keep you here overnight and re-evaluate you in the morning. I know you want to go home, but I think you suffered a mild concussion and you need to be monitored. Oh, and no visitors until the morning. Now, now," he said when Sarah started to object, "No arguments. I'm confident you'll be fine in the morning. I've prescribed a mild pain killer that will help with the headache, so if you need more, just ring the duty nurse."

Sarah didn't answer, just nodded her head and closed her eyes.

Nico arrived at the hospital an hour later, after being called by Detective Colby while he was driving back to the city. Afternoon traffic and a jack-knifed big rig delayed him for over an hour and a half. All his relentless pleading and his considerable charm finally wore down the duty nurse. She allowed him five minutes, cautioning him that if Sarah was sleeping, he was not to wake her.

"I promise. Five minutes only and I won't wake her. Thank you so much."

Nico entered Sarah's room quietly nodding to the officer sitting in a chair outside the door. "Hey, Dave," he said, "just gonna check on her."

"No sweat, Nico. Take your time,'" Dave replied, turning back to the paperback novel he had been reading.

Not wanting to disturb her if she was asleep, he sat next to her bed and just looked at her, not saying anything for a few minutes, just watching her sleep. He had been so worried about her when Detective Colby called he felt physically sick. The traffic jam and accident was maddening and by the time he arrived at the hospital, he had an awful headache. He reached out and took her hand, covering it with his, softly stroking it. He left fifteen minutes later.

Sarah wasn't released until the next day, late in the morning, after all the test results had been returned and the doctor had checked them. Nico came by to take her home, on the condition that she stay away from work for a couple of more days and just rest. Nico wheeled her out to the parking lot and helped her into his car, then drove carefully out of the parking lot.

***

As Nico drove away from the hospital, Jacob was walking down a street several blocks away. He looked just like any other person on his way to an appointment or to meet a friend. He was so ordinary appearing that no one took notice of him. Jacob didn't look left or right as he walked. He knew exactly where he was going and what time he needed to be there. Last night he realized his next client needed his services today. After his failed attempt to run down the woman cop, he dumped the stolen truck at the bus station and hurried home, afraid to leave his apartment until he had to go to work. That night, he accessed the records room and found his next client, an elderly woman, Helen Winston, suffering from congestive heart failure causing her to be wheelchair-bound and almost entirely an invalid.

According to her chart at the hospital, her personal assistant, an elder care worker hired by her daughter living in Arizona, would arrive around eight in the morning to help her out of bed and get her cleaned up. After fixing and serving her breakfast, she would do some light housekeeping and some laundry, then take her out for an hour or two, returning by lunchtime. She would fix her lunch, turn on the television, and while her patient was eating in front of the T.V., she would step out for an hour to run errands for her. It was during this time that Jacob decided to pay her a visit.

As he walked, he thought of the woman cop and how close he had come to eliminating her. He knew he had lost his advantage and that another attack on her was a bad idea. She would be on her guard, as would the other cops around her. He needed another diversion, one they wouldn't expect, one that would divert their attention from his work. He was so distracted by his thoughts, he didn't notice the person following him.

As he approached the house, he could see the care worker's car still in the driveway. He slowed as he started to pass by, trying to see inside the house, not knowing if the old lady was alone or if the care worker was still there. As he passed, he couldn't tell one way or the other, so he walked past the house for a block, then turned around and walked back. Knowing there was a small branch library two blocks away, he walked up the porch and knocked on the front door. After a short moment, the door was opened by the care worker.

"Hello, can I help you?" she asked.

"Yes, please. I am looking for the branch library. I know it's close by, but I think I made a wrong turn a block or so back. Do you know where it is?"

"Oh, yes. Go down one more block and turn right. At the next street, turn left and it will be a half-block down."

Jacob thanked her and left the porch, walking in the direction of the library, disappointed that he would have to wait for another day.

The man following him crossed the street to a small park and sat at one of the tables there, partially screened by some shrubbery and watched the house for the next thirty minutes. When he was sure the care worker would not be leaving anytime soon, he got up and started back toward his hotel. He mumbled softly to himself as he walked with his head down, causing passers-by to glance at him and give him a little wider berth as they passed.

Chapter 11

S arah awoke the next morning feeling refreshed though still a bit sore. The headache was tolerable and she was famished, having not eaten anything solid over the last two days. She stretched, then sat up in bed. Swinging her feet off the bed, she gingerly stood up, not trusting her balance to stand too quickly. When she didn't feel any dizziness, she smiled and walked to the bedroom door. She went into the living room and was momentarily startled to see a figure lying on her couch, covered with an old afghan she kept folded over the back. She remembered Nico saying he would stay the night on the couch and smiled to herself.

She walked quietly to the couch and leaned over, kissing him gently on the cheek, then shook his shoulder and said, "Nico, wake up. It's morning."

Nico grunted and turned onto his back. He opened his eyes and looked around, briefly disoriented by his surroundings. He felt uneasy, out of sorts. He remembered dreaming, but not what the dream was about. He only knew it was disturbing and that there was a shadowy figure that seemed to be dressed all in black involved. Spotting Sarah standing over him, he smiled and said, "Good morning." He sat up and ran his hands through his hair and asked, "How're you feeling today?"

"Fine. A little sore but the headache is gone. You hungry?"

"Starving. What's for breakfast?"

"Well, since I wasn't expecting guests, how about something from Abe's Diner down the block?"

"That's OK with me. I need to use the facilities."

"Go ahead. There's a clean towel in the cabinet behind the door." Sarah turned and headed toward her bedroom, stopping at the door way, she turned around and said, "Oh, and don't forget, this is a woman's home, so make sure the toilet seat is down when you are done."

Two hours later, they had eaten breakfast and returned to the apartment. Nico made sure Sarah was comfortable and made her promise not to go to work, even going so far as refusing to leave until she called the police department and her office to let them know. They made plans to meet in a few hours at Nico's office to go over some ideas on what to do next. Nico was worried about her safety. Knowing it was very likely there had already been one attempt on her life, he was reluctant to leave her alone for long. He suspected that whoever had tried to harm her would try again, and he wanted to be close by to protect her. As he left, he warned her to keep her door locked and not to open it to strangers.

After Nico left, Sarah locked the door and checked the windows to make sure they were latched. She hadn't wanted to say anything in front of him, but she, too, was concerned about her safety. She worried that whoever had tried to run her down was still out there and, like Nico, felt there could be another attempt on her life.

When she was satisfied that everything was locked, she went to her bedroom and took one of the painkillers the doctor had prescribed. She had lied to Nico when she told him the headache was gone, and she was a bit more than a "little" sore. Though her headache was more of a nuisance than a problem her bruises hurt more as she healed.

She unlocked the small gun safe on the top shelf of the closet and took out her hand gun. Checking that there was a fully loaded magazine in it, she pulled the slide back, chambering a round, then snapped the safety on and carried it with her into the living room. She lay down on the couch and covered up with the blanket she kept there. The gun was under the blanket next to her where she could quickly and easily grab it if needed.

As she lay on the couch, she went over the investigation in her mind trying to figure out what she had done that had caused someone to try to kill her. She knew the attempt had to be related to the investigation and that she might be getting close to the suspect, but for the life of her she didn't know what is was that worried him. After a few minutes the pain-killer kicked in and she dozed off. She slept peacefully.

Nico drove to the police department and asked to talk with Detective Colby. He was told that Colby was in a meeting at the moment but would be done in a few minutes, and if he wished, he could take a seat in the lobby and wait. After fifteen minutes, a clerk came out and told him Colby was free and would see him. She led him past the security door and down the hallway to his office. As he entered, he saw Colby was on the phone. Colby waved him to a chair next to his desk and held up a finger to indicate he would be done in a moment.

"Yes, I do realize that, but at this time, we have very little to go one." He listened for a few moments then said, "No, no plate, and the witnesses were no help. The best we can do is that it was an older, beat-up Ford pickup truck. We are researching stolen vehicle reports in the county, but so far no luck. Ok, I'll keep in touch." He hung up the phone and stood up, reaching across his desk to shake Nico's hand.

"What can I do for you, professor?" he asked, sitting back down.

"Please, call me Nico. I just wanted to talk with you about Sarah," Nico replied. "I'm worried about her safety."

"Yeah, we are too. That was the chief of the campus police telling me the same thing and asking whether we had any information as to who tried to run her down."

"Well, are you guys making any progress?"

"You heard what I told him, didn't you, about the truck? Very little useful information. Even I didn't get a good look at it. I was more occupied with pulling her out of the way, and by the time I could look up, he had already turned a corner and was out of sight."

"So, was anyone able to describe the driver?"

"One witness who was driving in the next lane caught a glimpse of him as he drove past her, but it happened so fast she was unable to provide much info, other than it was a white male with dark hair between the ages of forty and fifty-five. Not much help there." Lieutenant Colby leaned forward and said, "We are looking into this as an attempted murder, Nico, and will do our very best to find out who did it. Sarah is one of our own, another cop, and we take these things personally."

"I know you do, Lieutenant."

"I've called for a lot of extra patrol around her place with frequent drive-bys. If this creep is trying to get to her, that should discourage him from trying anything at her apartment. I'll call her later and ask if she wants an escort to work for the next few days. I can have a patrol car meet her at her place and escort her in, but from what I've seen, she won't agree to that," he said, grinning.

Nico smiled back, "You're right, she won't. I plan to drive her in and take her home for the next few days. I know she won't like it, but the doctor told her to take her medications regularly for a couple of days to handle the headaches and body aches, and that means she can't drive. I'll make sure she gets here safely."

"Thanks, Nico. That will be a big help, and a relief. Is there anything else I can do for you?" Colby asked.

Nico stood up and said, "No, Sir. If there is anything else you need from me just let me know."

"I will, Nico, Take care."

Nico went to his office and spent a couple of hours finishing up cleaning and closing his office. On the way home he stopped at a small diner and grabbed a quick dinner, then went home. After showering and changing his clothes he called his mother to let her know about Sarah and her close brush with death. After he had told her and assured her Sarah was OK, the conversation turned to the murder investigation.

"I keep feeling there is something familiar about this. I've tried to think of what it is, but nothing comes to mind. There've been times that something has come over me, where I've felt sick, dizzy, and I know it's related to the case, but I don't know how or why it affects me that way."

There was a few moments of silence on the other end of the line, then his mother asked, "Tell me again, Nico, about the dark figure you saw that night, the first time you felt ill."

Thinking it odd, Nico wondered why she wanted to know that. "Why, Ma? Is it important?"

"Yes, son. I have an idea as to what's bothering you, but I want to make sure before I say anything."

"OK. Well, as I said, he was just a dark figure, dressed all in black. I believe he had a long cape on and a tall hat, like an Abe Lincoln hat, too, but I can't be positive about that."

"Were there any bread crumbs on the body?"

"Yes. How did you know that?"

"That confirms my suspicions, Nico. Now, I don't know if you really did see the person I am about to tell you about, but I know why you saw what you did." Sighing deeply she continued, asking, "Do you remember your grandfather, Nico?"

"Sure I do, Ma. We had a lot of good times together."

"He loved you very much you know, like you were his own son."

"I know. I loved him, too."

"Do you remember the day he died, what happened that day?"

"Not really. I just remember the family being at the house and everyone was crying. I remember us going into the bedroom to say goodbye, and then being back in the parlor with Aunt Helen and the family. Did something happen?"

"Is that all you remember, Honey?"

"Yes. What else was there?"

"You don't remember there was a man there, in the room? A man dressed all in black?"

Nico got up from the chair and walked to the window, looking out over the city, thinking hard. There it was again, a nagging thought that this was familiar.

"No, I don't. Who was this man? Was he part of the family?"

"No, Nico, not part of the family. He was asked to the house by your grandmother. He was a Sin Eater."

"A Sin Eater? Really? I didn't know anyone still believed in them, much less used them."

"Apparently your grandparents did, and called for him when your grand dad was dying. He terrified you. So much so I had to take you out of the room. You nearly passed out and had nightmares for weeks afterwards. After all, you were only six."

Realization crossed Nico's features, as if a veil had been lifted. "I remember, Ma. He seemed to be so full of evil. I didn't understand what was going on back then and he terrified me." He turned away from the window, walked to the couch and sat down. "That's why I've been getting those feelings," he exclaimed. "Whenever I'm around him or where he has been, I can sense his presence!"

"I think so, Nico. You blocked the incident from your mind, it was so frightening."

"How long have you known, Ma?"

"I have suspected for a while, ever since you told me of seeing the man in the shadows. I wasn't sure until now."

"A Sin Eater! How could I have not realized it?"

"I think you buried it so deep, and it was so traumatic, your subconscious wouldn't let you remember."

"Ma, I gotta go. I've got to let Sarah know about this. Thanks, Ma, this is huge. I love you."

Her "I love you, too, Nico" fell on deaf ears as he had already disconnected the call.

Ten minutes later, Nico was ringing Sarah's doorbell, waking her up. Sarah sat up, her pistol in her hand. She snapped the safety off and called out, "Who's there?" When she heard Nico say, "It's me, Nico. I need to tell you something," she got up and opened the door. Nico saw the gun she carried and said, "Whoa, Sarah, what's with the gun?"

"Oh!" she exclaimed, "Sorry Nico. Just being careful."

"Good, Sarah, glad you're taking this seriously."

"Come in," she said, closing the door behind him as he entered.

Nico crossed quickly to the couch and sat down, patting the cushion next to him. "Here, sit down. I've got something important to tell you."

Sarah flipped the safety back on, put the gun on the coffee table and sat down next to Nico. "So, what's up?"

Chapter 12

Twenty minutes later Sarah, an incredulous look on her face, sat back in the couch, speechless, as Nico told her, "...and thanks to my mother, I now know why I have been getting those queasy, unsettling feelings every once in a while. It must be when I'm close to him that it happens." Sarah sat there in silence for a half a minute, looking out the window behind him. "Sarah? Did you hear me?"

She looked at him and said, "Yes, Nico, I heard you."

"So where do we go from here? Should we call Inspector Colby and tell him? What about your chief?"

She thought for a moment, sighed and looked at him. "Nico, how can I take this to the inspector or anyone else connected to the case? They would laugh me out of the room!"

"But, Sarah, we need to let someone know! This is important information. We have a lead on the suspect!"

She took his hand in hers before telling him, "I'm having a tough time believing it, Nico, and I care for you. Imagine what their reaction would be." She let go of his hand and got up from the couch, walking to the window and looked out for a few moments. "No, what we need to do is get some real information about this Sin Eater, something solid about who he is. Once we have that, we can give it to Lieutenant Colby and he'll take it from there."

"And in the meantime what do we do? Just wait for him to murder someone else?"

Turning back to Nico, Sarah replied, "Of course not. We have to dig deeper. There is a link we are missing, Nico, a link between our suspect and the victim.

Our victim was not picked at random. Something made him choose the professor and I'm pretty sure it was his terminal illness. We need to find out how he knew about it, what the link between them was. Once we know the why, we will find the who."

"OK, so how do we go about it?"

"Well, first off, there's not going to be a 'we' in this anymore. Colby already warned me about having you involved in the investigation. If he knows we are still working together, I could lose my job."

"C'mon, Sarah, I have to help you find him. Don't you see? He and I are connected. I can feel when he is around and where he has been. You have to admit that could be a huge help to you, right?"

Sarah just looked at him, realizing he was right. How could she not use his help when he was so dialed in to the suspect? It just might give them an edge. "OK, Nico, you can help, but we can't be seen together a lot. We'll keep in touch by cell phone and meet once a day, briefly."

Nico smiled, relieved. "Thanks, Sarah. What do you want me to do?"

"For starters, get me some background on Sin Eaters, what they do, when they do it. You know, all the basics."

"What are you gonna be doing while I'm on the computer?"

"I'll be doing some research on other deaths in the valley that could be linked."

"How will you know, Sarah? You already checked for similar cases with no results."

"This time I'll be looking for any suspicious deaths, not just other homicides. Maybe something will turn up that will help. We'll see. I'm going to make some calls to the larger cities and see if they've had any deaths that might fit the bill. I think I'll start with all the cities with a population greater than 25,000 between Bakersfield and Fresno."

"Why those particular ones, Sarah?"

"Most cities with less than that in population are unlikely to have their own police department, and even if they did, their County Sheriff's would most likely handle any major investigations."

"Well, I wish you luck. What will you do if you don't get any useful information?"

"Then I will start calling the Sheriff's Departments." She put her hand on Nico's, "I've got a good feeling about this, Nico. I think it will lead us to our killer, but I want you to do one thing for me, OK?"

"Sure, Sarah, anything."

"I want you to be very careful. Now don't take this the wrong way, but you need to pay more attention to your surroundings and people around you."

"What do you mean?"

"It's just that at times you seem to be in your own little world, totally oblivious to your surroundings. This guy that tried to run me down might have more than one target in mind so please, be careful, OK?"

"OK." Nico gently squeezed her hand, touched and pleased that Sarah showed so much concern for him. He stood up and cleared his throat, "I better get going. Got a lot of research to do."

Sarah stood and walked him to the door. "Give me a call in a few hours. Maybe we can meet later today?"

"Sure. Well, talk to you later."

Before he could turn to leave, Sarah grabbed him by the shoulders and kissed him fully on the mouth. Taken by surprise, his response was one of shock, but he quickly responded, kissing her back passionately. "Wow!" he exclaimed, once the kiss ended.

"Yeah," Sarah replied, "Wow. You better get going," breaking the embrace and backing off a step. "We've got a killer to catch."

Nico turned and walked into the hallway toward the exit. He stopped at the main door and turned, raising his hand to wave goodbye but saw that her door was already closed.

A half hour later Nico was in his office at the computer reading about sin eaters. He knew a bit about the custom but was fascinated to learn that there were several versions of the lore, depending on the culture involved. He found that the sin eater ritual was practiced mostly in England and Scotland for hundreds of years and was thought to have died out by the late 19th century. Some scholars and historians put the date later, into the early 20th century, and there are even believers that swear the ritual is still practiced to this day. In America, sin eaters were common in Appalachia through the end of the 19th century.

In earlier times, the sin eater would perform the ritual over the corpse which had been laid out on a bier. He would be given a loaf of bread and a bowl of ale, and sometimes a payment in coin, or would take coins placed on the eyelids of the deceased. Thus he would not only get paid for his service but would receive a meal at the same time. In later times the ritual was usually performed over a dying person at their home, the family having summoned him.

The ritual itself symbolized the sin eater taking on the burden of the deceased or dying person's sins, thereby absolving his or her soul and allowing that person to rest in peace. In some cultures, it was considered a service to the living also, as the absolution of sins not only saved the person from hell but kept them from wandering the earth as a ghost.

Nico found, not to his surprise, that the Roman Catholic Church would often excommunicate the sin eater when they were more common, not only because of the excessive sins they carried, but also because they infringed on the territory and functions of the priests who were supposed to administer Last Rites to the dying according to church doctrine.

Nico leaned back in his chair for a few minutes and thought of what he had learned. He knew as well as Sarah that if they found out the killer was indeed a sin eater then their next problem would be figuring out how he selected his victims. Of the two recent murders, only one, the professor, was terminally ill. Though Donna Lapin's murder was definitely connected to the professor's, he still didn't know why she was targeted. What did she know that was so important the killer felt she was a danger to him? He was anxious to talk to Sarah to learn if she had found any other murders that could be connected with theirs. He looked at his watch and realized it had only been two hours since he had left her apartment. He sighed and stood up, stretching the kinks out of his joints. He realized he was hungry and set off for the cafeteria for some lunch, so occupied with his thoughts that he forgot to lock his office.

He watched Nico as he left the building, heading toward the cafeteria. Once he was sure Nico would not be back any time soon, he walked to Nico's building and headed down the hall toward his office. He had slung an old backpack over his shoulders and dressed in levis and a faded t-shirt, he was indistinguishable from the dozens of other students walking around the campus. He looked around as he approached Nico's office door and saw there was no one else in the hallway. He was surprised when he tried the door and found it was unlocked. He was prepared to tell anyone inside the office that he was looking for another professor whose office was actually three doors down. He saw the small office was empty and quickly slipped inside, locking the door behind him. He began his search by checking the drawers of the desk, then moved to the file cabinet. Neither had much in them so after a few minutes he was certain there was nothing of interest there and moved to the computer. He pressed the enter key and the screen came back to life from "sleep" mode. Nico hadn't deleted the last webpage and he was startled to see the information about sin eaters on the screen. He was alarmed that Nico knew, or suspected, that the murders were committed by a sin eater. He knew he would have to take a stronger approach to this, that he was almost to the point where he would have to take some drastic action. It disturbed him and he felt torn between doing what should be done and doing what he wanted to do. He left the office quietly and walked out of the building, heading off the campus, deep in thought. Halfway back to his room, he changed direction and set off for Helen Winston's house, feeling the need to see if she was alone and unprotected.

Chapter 13

When Nico got back to his office, he was surprised to find the door unlocked. Smiling to himself, he thought he must have really been distracted to forget to lock it. He quickly looked around as he entered and, seeing nothing out of place, thought no more about it.

He spent the next hour straightening up his office, then packed his battered valise with the sin eater info he printed from the computer and left, this time carefully locking his door. When he got home, he called Sarah and told her he had some information she should see. They agreed to meet at her place in an hour.

Nico still did not feel like himself. He was tired and uneasy and felt like he needed a shower. He went to the bathroom, stripped off his clothes and stepped into the shower. Turning the water on high, he set the temperature to as hot as he could stand it and just stood under it with his eyes closed for a good five minutes. He lathered up and washed thoroughly and rinsed off. Turning off the shower, he stepped out and grabbed his towel, draping it over his head like a hood. Grabbing the sides if the sink, he leaned forward and looked in the fog covered mirror, seeing only his blurred image. He closed his eyes and hung his head. He felt better and his spirits began to rise. Standing up, still with his eyes closed, he dried his hair, pulled the towel from his head and opened his eyes, looking in the still fogged mirror. He could see his blurred reflection and, to his shock, the image of a black clothed figure standing behind him.

His heart racing, he quickly turned around and saw there was no one there. Looking back in the mirror, his image was all he could see. He took a deep breath, trying to slow his pounding heart, wondering if he was hallucinating.

Stop it! he thought to himself. *There's no one there. There never was. It's just your imagination.* He shook his head and walked into his bedroom. Dressing quickly, he combed his hair, grabbed his valise, and left for Sarah's, still feeling uneasy over the image in the mirror.

"I swear, Sarah," he was telling her as they sat on her couch, "It was really weird. It looked so real but when I turned around, there was no one there. Really creeped me out."

"You were just seeing things, Nico," she replied. "Just a case of an over active imagination."

"You're probably right," Nico admitted, smiling at her.

Nico knew it wasn't just his imagination. He felt a tenuous connection between him and the Sin Eater, a connection that became more apparent each day. It was stronger whenever Nico was in the same place he had been, or, though Nico didn't know it, whenever he was close by.

He tried to process what his mother had told him, to put it in its proper perspective. He was not having much luck. The more he thought of the Sin Eater, the more uneasy he became. In his latest dreams he felt as if they were looking through the same eyes, seeing the same things. He would get flashes of faces and buildings, though it was always a quick picture and nothing he could recognize. The faces seemed to be twisted in fear or agony. He wasn't sure which, but he did feel the eyes he was looking through belonged to a predator. He was never able to see his face, only what he saw.

Lost in his thoughts, he didn't realize Sarah was talking, asking him something. "Sorry, Sarah, were you asking me something?"

"Yes, Nico. Three times! Where were you, 'cause you certainly weren't here?"

"I've just got a lot on my mind lately. I haven't been sleeping well."

"Is that really all it is, Nico? You had such a frown on your face just now. What's really going on?"

Nico turned to her and took her hands in his. He sighed and said, "I don't know, Sarah. I can't figure it out, these dreams I'm having. It's like I see everything he sees, but there's nothing I recognize. No faces, no places. And I don't know why he is doing these things. I think that's what's bothering me most."

"Look, Nico. Why don't you stay here tonight? If you dream of him again, maybe we can get something else that could lead us to him. What do you say?"

Nico grinned at her and said, "I don't know. That couch of yours is not very comfortable. Maybe that's one of the reasons I'm not sleeping well."

Sarah Smiled back at him and took his hand. "Well, the bed is pretty comfortable." She turned and, still holding his hand, gently pulled him toward the bedroom.

***

He left his hotel room and walked toward the diner, feeling the need for food and coffee. Mostly coffee. He walked quickly, looking side to side with an occasional glance behind him. He had a feeling that someone was closing in on him, that he was in danger. He pulled the brim of his hat down, and walked faster. When he got to the diner, he sat at his usual table. He ordered toast, unbuttered, and black coffee. He took his hat off and placed it on the seat next to him and ran his fingers through his thinning hair, smoothing it down.

The coffee was hot and strong and tasted good. He started to calm down and after a few minutes was able to take a few bites of the toast. He realized he was hungrier than he thought and waved the waitress over, asking for more coffee and ordering two fried eggs and a slice of ham. When the food arrived, he ate quickly, washing it down with the lukewarm coffee. He felt better after eating, calmer. He sipped the last of his coffee as he looked out the diner window, scanning the street out front. Night had fallen and there were few people walking around.

He put money on the table and left the diner, walking aimlessly down the street. As he walked, he again got the distinct feeling he was being watched. He looked quickly behind him, seeing no one there, though out of the corner of his eye he thought he saw the wisp of a shadow slip quickly into an alley a half a block away. He continued his stroll and the longer he walked, the more uneasy he became. Each time he looked behind him he saw no one and no shadows. He knew what it meant. He needed to find another client to help, and soon. As his restlessness grew, his walk became a hunt.

Nico was sleeping fitfully, dreaming. He could see a Formica table with dirty dishes and an empty coffee cup on it, then the scene jumped to a view of a street as he walked down it. He could see the buildings as he passed, but none looked familiar to him. He felt unsettled, nervous, and a yearning came over him. As he passed a storefront window he caught a glimpse of himself. He was startled to see he was wearing a black suit and appeared to be much older. There were thoughts running through his head that disturbed him. He felt he needed to find someone for some purpose he couldn't quite discern, though he knew for certain it was an evil purpose. He realized he walked with a purpose, turning down a side street and into a neighborhood of small homes.

Nico felt as if he was watching a movie of himself. He saw the houses as he passed them, crossing other streets, walking deeper into the neighborhood. He seemed to be moving with a singular purpose, as if he had found what he was looking for. He seemed to be walking faster now, and Nico could see a small yellow cottage with a red door in the distance. His spirits seemed to rise as he approached and he felt calmer the closer he got to the house.

The next view in the dream was as him walking up to the front porch toward the red door. Nico could see the house number 167 on the wall, and as he reached the door, it opened. As he stepped inside, he felt a wave of relief. He made his way through the small house to the bedroom, halting before the closed door. An evil power seemed to be flowing through him as he reached for the doorknob, a power he was familiar with, a comforting power. He knew he would soon get the relief he needed through the terror and death of the person behind the door. As he turned the knob and started to open the door, a strong feeling of loathing washed over him causing him to awake with a start. He sat up quickly in the bed, sweating profusely, his heart racing.

"Nico?" Sarah asked, "What's going on?"

Nico looked at her and said, "Sorry I woke you, Sarah."

"You're all sweaty! Are you feeling all right?"

"I'm fine. Just had a bad dream." Nico fought the nausea he felt, not wanting to alarm Sarah.

"Was it about the Sin Eater?" she asked, sitting up quickly, rubbing her eyes and yawning. She looked at the bedside clock and saw it the 4:34 in the morning.

"Yes, only this one was more vivid."

Sarah threw back the covers and got out of bed, grabbing her robe, she said, "I'll make some coffee and we can talk about it, OK?"

"OK," Nico replied, wiping the perspiration from his face with his hand. "I'm going to throw some water on my face. Meet you in the other room in a couple of minutes."

Nico and Sarah were sitting on the couch sipping their coffee. Nico hadn't said anything since he came out of the bathroom. He was still disturbed by the dream and took the time to calm down.

"So, Nico, want to tell me about it?" Sarah asked.

Nico took a deep breath and started talking, looking down at his hands holding the coffee cup. "It was much more vivid than the others," he said. "It was like I could see through his eyes, and I could feel what he was feeling." He looked up at Sarah and said, "I felt such evil in him, Sarah, and it was an awful feeling."

"What did you see, Nico? Anything you recognized?"

"No, nothing."

"Start from the beginning of the dream and tell me everything. Don't leave out anything, no matter how insignificant it might seem."

"Ok. The first thing I remember is seeing a small table with an empty coffee cup on it. It could have been a coffee shop or diner somewhere. The table was a light green, like formica."

Sarah asked, "Did you see a name or something else that might identify it?"

"No, just the cup and the table."

"OK. Then what did you see?"

"The next thing was him walking along a sidewalk. He was very nervous, kept looking behind him as if he was afraid someone was following him. He was walking along past some stores and I could see his reflection in one of the windows as he passed it."

Sarah took a sip from of her coffee. "Let me guess. Black suit and hat? White shirt, black tie?"

"That's him. He looked older. I couldn't see any specific facial features, but I felt he was somewhere around sixty years old. God, Sarah," Nico said, taking a deep breath, "There was such menace and evil emanating from him. I've never felt anything like that before."

Sarah put her cup down, turned to Nico and gently took his hand in hers. "Why would you have, Nico? That's not you. You were connected to him in some way, feeling what he was feeling. You are not like him and you've got to remember that."

"I know that, Sarah, but it's so hard for me."

"Try to forget about that part, Nico. Let's talk about what else you saw," Sarah asked, trying to change the subject.

"Well. I remember walking through a residential neighborhood, looking at the houses along the way as if I was searching for something or someone. I felt calmer, and a strange anticipation was starting to grow in my head."

Sarah caught the change in Nico's narrative. He was now talking as if he was describing his own actions, not someone else's.

"As I walked, I saw a yellow house, no, more like a cottage, in the distance. I started to feel better the closer I got to it."

"That's good, Nico. We have something identifiable to focus on. A yellow house! What else did you see? Did you get close to the house?"

"I did. I remember it had a red door!" Nico said, gazing at the floor. He turned to Sarah and grinned. "That's significant, isn't it?"

"Absolutely, Nico. There can't be many yellow houses with red doors in town. That will help narrow the search a bit. Only thing better would be the street name and house number," Sarah said with a rueful grin.

"167", Nico said. "I remember seeing the number 167 on the wall next to the door!" Nico exclaimed excitedly.

"Great," Sarah exclaimed. "Did you see the street name too?"

"No. Sorry."

"No problem. That's a huge help. Good job, Nico," Sarah said, throwing her arms around Nico's neck and hugging him.

"That's all I can remember, Sarah. I hope it's enough."

"I think it will be a huge help. We've got a place to start. I'll get the information on the house out to the patrol officers. Maybe we'll get lucky and one of them will recognize the house."

"Good. One other thing, Sarah. I had the distinct feeling that I was seeing what was yet to happen."

"Really? I was assuming you saw it as if it had already happened." Sarah got up from the couch and walked to the window. "Damn!" she exclaimed, "That puts a new wrinkle into the investigation."

"How so?" Nico asked. "I would think it's a good thing. If it hasn't happened yet, we may be able to stop it."

"True, but we don't know when it's going to happen. Could be a week from now, could be tonight." She turned back to Nico and said, "I've got to call the police department and get them on this right away. What time is it?" she asked, looking at her watch. "Shit, its four fifty in the morning. Lieutenant Colby isn't going to like this. Nico, I need you to go now. Get dressed while I make the call. I'll need to go in to work, so I'll call you when I can, OK?"

"All right. I'll be at my apartment," Nico said to her back as she walked to into the kitchen dialing the phone.

Chapter 14

S arah had arrived at the police department a half hour after calling in asking the dispatcher to call Lieutenant Colby and tell him to contact her. He called her a few minutes later and she was able to convince him that they needed to act on her information immediately. She sipped her coffee as she sat in the conference room waiting for him to arrive, talking to the graveyard watch commander and three of the patrol officers about the small house Nico had seen in his dream.

She didn't tell them where she got the information, only that an anonymous caller had provided it an hour ago. She knew they would not believe her if she told them how she really had learned about it and knew it would hurt her credibility in the department. Most of the officers already did not believe she could be of any help to them because she was merely a "campus cop" and a wannabe real cop. They had little respect for her and didn't want her help.

They all said they hadn't come across a house of that description and the information about the coffee shop and street was so sketchy that it could be any of two dozen neighborhoods in the city and surrounding areas. Sarah was losing hope that they would be able to find the house in time to do whatever needed to be done to capture the suspect or, perhaps, to save whoever lives there.

"This better be good, Officer Ferris," Lieutenant Colby stated as he walked into the room. "It's way too early for you to be wasting my time, so let's hear whatever it is you have to say." Turning to the officers he barked, "Would it be too much to ask someone to get me some coffee?" The Sergeant nodded at one of the officers who hurriedly left for the coffee room.

"So," Lieutenant Colby said, "What's so important about this information that we needed to meet at this ungodly hour?"

Sarah took a deep breath and began telling him what she had learned from Nico. She talked for the next few minutes, leaving out only Nico's involvement, trying to convince them that this could be the break they were looking for.

"So if we can find that house before anything happens, we can be a step ahead of the suspect. Maybe we could set up surveillance on it, maybe catch him in the act?"

"All well and good, Officer Ferris, but what assurances do we have that the information is good and that whatever it is hasn't happened yet?" Lieutenant Colby asked.

"No assurances, Lieutenant, but I know in my heart that it is good info and that for whatever reason we got it before anything happens. I know it, Sir."

Lieutenant Colby sat silent for a short time, his fingers tapping the table top while he thought about what Sarah had told them.

"OK, let's start looking for this yellow house with the red door." Turing to the watch commander he instructed, "Get together with all of your officers and have them start an active search of their beat. Concentrate on any houses or buildings numbered 167. But don't limit the search just to those. We still don't know if it's good info or not, but it won't hurt to be a bit proactive with this. Let's treat it as if the information is good and go from there."

Looking at his watch he said, "It's two hours before shift change. Sergeant, tell the dispatcher to call in the day shift clerks immediately. Once they get here, have them do a search of the reverse directory and our records for all houses with the number 167 and compile a list for the day shift crew." Turning to Sarah he said, "Is there any way you can contact this anonymous caller? Maybe to find out any other info he may have?"

"I don't know, Sir. I'm hoping he will call back soon. If he does, I'll find out if there is anything else he can tell us."

"Well, I guess that will have to do for now." Turning back to the Sergeant he said, "I'll be here if you need to contact me. If anyone comes across a house with that description, let me know right away."

The Sergeant replied, "OK. LT," and left the room, pulling his portable radio from his belt holder to call the rest of the beat officers.

Once they were alone, Lieutenant Colby turned to Sarah and said, "For the time being, I'll go along with your 'anonymous caller' explanation, but I've got to tell you, that just doesn't make much sense."

Sarah's heart skipped a beat at this, but she hid her surprise well. "What do you mean, Sir?"

"I mean I'm not buyin' it. First of all, if the person was really an anonymous caller, how did he get your home phone number? And how would he know to call you? Why not call the police department instead? No, I don't think it came from an anonymous caller. You're protecting someone and I have an idea who that may be. Now, I'm not gonna press it. You can have your little secret for now, but at some point you will have to tell me the truth, OK?"

Sarah knew her little deception hadn't worked and said, "Yes Sir." Changing the subject she said, "Can I get you some more coffee?"

"Yes, thank you. You can help the clerk up front with the address search when you're done."

"Yes, Sir," she replied, as she left the room.

***

Two hours after he had left Sarah's, Nico paced the small living room in his apartment, sipping coffee, too charged up to sleep. He had shaken off the negative effects of the dream and his mind was racing from all he had seen through the eyes of the Sin Eater. He was feeling anxious about what he'd felt during the dream. He had a feeling of what he would have seen had he not woken up when he did. He might have witnessed a murder. What really bothered him was he had no idea who the victim was, or why they were targeted. He had chosen not to tell Sarah this as he couldn't be sure that would have been the outcome. He worried he was missing something and for the umpteenth time ran through the dream in his head, hoping to remember something new. After another half hour of agonizing over it, he finally lay down on the couch, exhausted.

The dream began with him seeing a man watching him from the house with the red door. He could feel the fear emanating from him, that he was in grave danger at this house, that someone nearby was a threat to him. He could feel the man's confusion, his uncertainty. He needed to hide for a while, to hopefully lose whoever it was watching him. In the dream, he began to run from the house, into the shadows and out of sight of the watcher. The dream faded and he sighed in his sleep, dropping deeper into a dreamless rest.

In another part of town, Jacob was just falling asleep despite his best efforts to stay awake. He slept soundly and did not dream.

***

Sarah knocked on Lieutenant Colby's door and entered carrying a sheaf of printouts.

"Excuse me Lieutenant, I've got some results from the address search."

Colby swiveled his chair around to face Sarah. "Good. Let's hear it," he said, leaning back.

Sarah walked to the side of his desk and sat in the other chair, placing the stack of paper on the corner of his desk. "Well, I've researched all the department's records and found only six references to residences numbered 167. Two references were from the same house, so that means there actually are just five houses in the database with that number."

"Thank you Officer Ferris, but I am well versed in simple mathematics," Colby replied, smiling at her. "Has anyone gone by them yet to see if any are yellow with a red door?"

"Not yet, Sir. I just finished and wanted to let you know the results."

"Good. I'll have dispatch send an officer by the addresses to take a look. Hopefully we will get lucky on this and find the house quickly, but somehow I don't think it's going to be that easy."

"OK. One of the dayshift clerks just got in and is starting an additional hand search of the city reverse directory for all houses with the 167 address."

"Can't that be done by computer?"

"I don't know. She didn't bring it up. I'll ask her before she gets too far into the search."

"Don't bother, Sarah. I know her well and if it was possible to use the computer, she would. She's very computer literate. I was just messing with you."

Sarah forced a slight smile and said, "Oh, OK. Had me going there for a moment. Well, I'll get back to work. I'll let you know the results of our search as soon as I can." She turned and walked quickly out of the office, angry with herself and slightly embarrassed for being so gullible.

The patrol officers had been sent to each of the five known 167 addresses to check them out. All reported none were painted yellow or had a red door.

Chapter 15

Three hours later Nico woke from his nap, refreshed and ready to again begin trying to figure out the dream. He made a fresh pot of coffee, poured a cup and added his usual teaspoon of sugar. Carrying it into the living room, he sat on the couch and dialed Sarah's cell phone.

"Hey Nico, good morning," she answered. "How'd the last few hours go? Are you feeling OK?"

"Yeah, I am. I managed to get a bit of sleep."

"Good. Wish I could say the same. We've been hard at work trying to find the house you saw in your dream."

"I take it you've been unsuccessful?"

"So far. We found several homes with an address of 167 but after checking them out, none are the house we are looking for. We are still searching for the right one and I'm confident we will eventually find it."

"I hope so, and soon. The one thing that bothers me most is that I don't know what he was up to and why he picked that house."

"Come on, Nico. I think you have an idea of why he was there, right?"

Nico paused for a couple of moments. His silence spoke volumes and Sarah said, "I thought so. I think we both know why he was there. I think it was to commit another murder."

"I do too. Damn, you're good."

"Yes, I am, and I can handle this stuff so next time don't try to protect me that way, OK?"

"OK. Sorry Sarah, it won't happen again."

"Alright. Now, have you thought of anything else? Something new from the dream?

"No, nothing yet. I've been thinking about it, going over the dream for hours, but so far nothing. It's driving me nuts because I don't know when the dream is supposed to happen. I hope it hasn't already, and if it hasn't, I hope we have enough time to figure this out. Since it was night time in my dream, we at least have the rest of this day. We need to stop him, Sarah, before he kills again."

"I know Nico. We're trying our best here. Listen, I gotta go. Got a meeting in about two minutes. I'll call you later. Call me if you think of anything. Oh, one last thing. During the search for the house one of the patrol officers located the pickup truck that almost ran me down."

"Really? That's good. Has it been impounded?"

"Yes. It's in the sally port of the department awaiting the evidence techs to process it. Hopefully they'll get something useful from it, like prints. Could be the break we were looking for. Anyway, gotta go. Bye, Nico."

Nico sat back on the couch and closed his eyes, remembering the dream more clearly this morning. Something about it was different. It was like he saw the same house from two different vantage points. Sometimes he was directly in front, other times off to one side and a bit further away. It was puzzling and he concentrated on the side view. He remembered he could see the house was yellow and the porch, but the door and address weren't in that view. He wondered about it for another minute, but dismissed it from his mind as unimportant. It obviously was the same house, just from a different view point. Probably just a fragment of the Sin Eater's mind from another time he was there.

Nico continued to review the dream but couldn't find anything new in his memory. He finally gave up, grabbed his car keys and left to find some breakfast.

He watched Nico drive away from his apartment and started the rental car. Pulling out into traffic, he kept a couple of cars between them. He followed Nico as he drove into the downtown area and parked in front of a small diner. He watched as he went inside and sat at the counter.

He parked a half a block away and walked back to the diner. A garish orange and pink neon sign shouted out Sally's Diner to all passers-by. He went in and sat at a table down from Nico, where he could watch him without seeming to do so.

Nico was sipping his coffee waiting for his breakfast to arrive, reading the paper. As he concentrated on the local news, he began to feel uneasy. The feeling of being watched washed over him, though it was different from the feeling he had in the dream. Though he felt a presence, it didn't feel threatening. He put the paper down and turned around, looking around the restaurant. There were several customers at the counter and several more at the tables in the dining room. All appeared to be engrossed in their own conversations, breakfasts, or newspapers. He got up and walked to the windows facing the sidewalk and looked up and down, and across, the street. Nothing and no one appeared out of place or unusual. Nico shrugged, took a deep breath, and walked back to the counter. The feeling had faded and he sat back down as his breakfast arrived.

Thirty minutes later Nico drained the last of the coffee from his cup. He picked up the bill and walked to the register. He gave the bill to the girl at the register. She looked at it and rang him up.

"That will be twelve fifty-five, Sir," she said.

As he dug in his pocket for his money, she added, "Oh, by the way, a man gave this to me and pointed you out, telling me to give it to you when you paid your bill." She handed him a small piece of note paper folded in half twice.

Nico took the paper and unfolded it and saw there were several hand printed lines on it. He quickly read what was written there. "Is the man still here?" he asked, knowing the answer.

"No, Sir. He gave it to me about fifteen minutes ago and left the diner."

"Have you seen him in here before?"

"No, I don't think so. I don't remember him ever being here."

"What did he look like?"

"Just like a regular guy, like most of the guys that come in here."

"I meant can you describe him?"

"Yeah, I suppose, but he was just a guy, nothing special about him."

"OK, but humor me and describe him, please."

"Well," she said, looking up toward the ceiling, thinking. "He was about your height and weight, and had brown hair. I'd say he was in his late thirties or so. Oh, yeah, he needed a shave too."

"He had a beard?"

"Not really. He just looked like he hadn't shaved in a few days."

"What about his clothing?" Nico asked.

"Levis, brown jacket, some sort of shirt under it. That's all I remember. I didn't really pay much attention to him," she said, smiling at Nico. "We were really busy when he gave the paper to me."

"That's OK. Listen, I'm giving you my cell number," Nico told her as he wrote the number on the back of his receipt. Handing it to her he said, "Please, give me a call if you remember anything else about him, or if he comes back in the diner, OK?"

"Sure," she replied, taking the receipt from him.

When Nico got back in his car he unfolded and reread the note, then immediately called Sarah and told her about it.

"What was written on it, Nico?"

"A warning for me to stay away. He wrote that he knew who I was. He called me Guardian, and said I should back away, that he would take any necessary action."

"Any necessary action? Action to do what?"

"I'd say to make sure I did what he said."

"Huh. Maybe so, but that's an odd way of putting it."

Nico gave her the man's description, saying, "It doesn't ring a bell with me. A bit too generic if you ask me, and too young for our suspect."

"Yeah, I know. Listen, I've gotta get back to a meeting with the detectives. I'll be done here in a couple of hours and I'll meet you at your place, OK?"

"OK, I'll wait for you there. What now, Sarah?"

"I'm going to talk to the LT, tell him about this note. Maybe he can put out a BOL for this guy, have the officers keep an eye out for him. Anyway, see you in an hour or so. And Nico, be careful."

Sarah hung up, went to the conference room and took her seat. Lieutenant Colby was addressing the other detectives and the on-duty Sergeant.

"I don't understand why we haven't identified this house yet. This town is not that big. What's the problem?"

No one spoke up and he turned to Sarah and asked, "Have you completed the records and cross directory search for the address, Sarah?"

"Yes Sir. No luck, though."

"Well, I guess this so-called tip from your so-called source isn't really much of a tip." Turning back to the room he said, "It's back to square one, guys. Let's get back to work and find this guy with real police work." He looked at Sarah and said, "You can call it day, Sarah," then turned and left the room, muttering under his breath.

Sarah felt her face burning with embarrassment as the other investigators walked from the room, avoiding looking at her as they passed by.

Chapter 16

N ico left the diner, walked across the street to his car and got in the driver's seat. He started the engine but just sat there, thinking about the note and that someone, possibly dangerous to him, was actually in the diner with him without his knowing it. An involuntary shudder rippled through him. He vowed to be more aware of his surroundings from now on.

He yawned and looked at his watch, seeing it was almost eleven in the morning. He was still feeling a bit drowsy from the lack of sleep the night before and the big breakfast. He leaned back in the seat and closed his eyes.

Something tenuous disturbed him and he sat up quickly, opening his eyes and looking around wildly. He saw houses and tree lined streets, not the businesses and shops by the diner. *How the hell did I get here?* He thought. *Where am I?*

Nico looked more slowly at his surroundings, seeing a neat and tidy residential neighborhood, the houses in good shape with freshly mowed lawns. It was getting dark outside and he wondered how much time had passed since he was at the diner. The clock on the dashboard showed it was nearing six in the evening. Nico was surprised and dismayed that he had no recollection of the last seven hours.

Scanning the neighborhood he got the distinct feeling what he was seeing was familiar. His gaze crossed one of the homes across the street and a flash of red caught his eye. He focused on the house and realized it was yellow and the front door was red. "Holy shit!" he exclaimed as he opened the car door and got out. Standing next to the car, he stared at the house, looking for movement or anything that seemed out of place. He stood there looking at it for a couple of minutes and knew deep inside that he had to go up to the house, that something wasn't right. That it was the house from his dream he had no doubt, and a growing feeling of dread began to worry him. He didn't feel there was any immediate danger to him, but his unease was disturbing.

He walked across the street and started up the walkway to the front door. He could see the address by the door, number 167. He climbed the three porch steps and walked to the front door. Looking at the numbers, he realized they didn't look right. The "1" and the "7" were in line, but the "6" was offset below the other two.

He reached up and touched the "6" and his touch started it rocking. Looking closer, he could see that the "6" was attached by just one small nail. He pushed and rotated it up until it was in line with the other two numbers and realized the address was actually 197. The top nail had fallen out allowing the number to swing down, making the address 167.

A lump was forming in his throat and the dread inside him continued to grow. He began to feel slightly nauseated. He grabbed the doorknob, took a deep breath, turned it and pushed the door open. As he took his first step into the living room, he knew he should have called Sarah. He should be waiting on the porch for her and the other police to arrive, but it seemed he couldn't control his actions. He *had* to enter the house.

He walked directly through the living room to the hallway, not pausing to look around and down the hallway to the last door on the right. He put his hand on the closed door and got a sudden flash of a person all in black, and a rush of evil.

The feeling was so strong he had to lean against the wall and take several breaths to clear his head and the dizziness that beset him. After a few moments, his head cleared and the nausea lessened. The feeling of evil faded and he stood up a bit taller, grasped the doorknob and entered, knowing what he would find.

Two hours later he was sitting on the top step of the porch while the investigators worked the scene for evidence. Sarah came out and sat next to him. She put her arm through his and leaned against him.

"You OK?" she asked.

Nico looked at her and nodded. "Yeah, I am. You know, Sarah, I knew what had happened in the house. I knew exactly where her body was and what the room looked like. The moment I touched the bedroom door, I got a flash. It was like I was watching a movie on fast forward." He paused for a short time and they sat there in silence. Sarah leaned her head on his shoulder and gently stroked his arm.

"You do know it was him, don't you?" Nico asked.

"Yes. When you told me you awoke parked across from the house, I knew it. The bond is getting stronger, Nico, and that frightens me."

He smiled at her and said, "I know. I can feel it, but that's a good thing, Sarah. I'm connecting with him quicker, and the things he sees are getting much clearer. Eventually we will know what he is planning and will be able to stop him." Nico took both her hands in his. "It's not a bad thing, Sarah. I know it's the way we will catch him." He sighed, and asked "So tell me about her. Why did he come after her?"

"Well, it seems she lived alone. No family nearby. Her only child, a son, lives in San Diego, but they haven't been in touch much the last ten years."

"Family problems?"

"I guess. We haven't called him yet, so your guess is as good as mine."

"Was she ill?" Nico asked.

"Yep, just like the professor. She had some pretty serious health issues and was taking a bunch of medications. Funny thing, though, as far as I can tell her condition wasn't a terminal situation. I'll know more when her doctor calls back."

Just then, Lieutenant Colby came out to the porch. "Sarah, I need you to start going door to door contacting the residents who are standing around outside watching us, or wake them up if you have to. Find out if they saw anyone lurking around here in the last few hours, or any activity around this house, OK? Get a description of anyone seen in the area."

"Sure, Lieutenant. I'll get right on it," she replied. "Gotta go Nico. See you later tonight?"

"Yeah. I'm going home now. Lieutenant Colby told me I was free to go once I gave my statement to the officers, so call me when you are done, alright?"

"I will." Sarah started to get up, then leaned over and kissed him on the cheek. "See you soon."

As Nico drove home he tried concentrating on the Sin Eater, trying to picture him in his mind, hoping he would get an idea of what he was up to or where he was, to no avail. All he could feel was a sense of relief and contentment from him.

Sarah watched him drive away, worried about him. There was something she didn't understand going on with him, something unusual. She hoped it wasn't a permanent state, that it would pass quickly.

"Sarah, we need to talk," Lieutenant Colby said as he walked up. "Follow me," he said and turned away, walking toward his car.

Sarah followed him, wondering what was going on with him. He opened the door for her and she slid onto the front seat. Once he got in the driver's side and closed the door he said, "Let's talk about your friend Nico."

"What about him," she asked, puzzled.

"How well do you know him?"

"Well enough. We've been friends for the last year. Why?"

"I'll get to that. Just bear with me for a bit. Now, again, how well do you know him, not how long. What do you know about his life, or his background? What does he do in his off time?"

"I know he lives alone. He has a small apartment a few blocks from the campus. He was raised by his mother and extended family. He was educated at UCLA, majoring in history. He doesn't have a very active social life as he is totally immersed in his teaching," she answered. "Why are you asking?"

"It's pretty obvious you two are closer than you would like people to know. I know you've been seeing each other on a social level, and from the signs, it appears you two are much closer that just friends."

Sarah didn't answer Colby's statement. She looked down at her hands, clasped in her lap and thought, *Damn, had they been that obvious? Were they too oblivious of their actions and demeanor towards to each other?*

She looked at him and admitted, "You're right. We have grown close since I started working on this case, but it hasn't interfered in the investigation, Lieutenant."

"I hope not, though I would bet he has information about it he shouldn't."

Sarah started to reply but Lieutenant Colby interrupted her by holding up his hand, palm out. "I don't care about that, Sarah. It's apparent he hasn't repeated anything he may have heard. No, my concern is that I have to strongly consider him a person of interest."

Sarah was shocked by this statement. "What? How could you possible think that?" she asked.

"I can because I'm not emotionally involved with him," he answered, giving her a knowing look. "Look, I know he is your source regarding the address of this house and suspect description, but I also know that he has no alibi for any of the murders."

"Oh, no, Lieutenant," she exclaimed. "He can't possibly be involved."

"Is that your heart talking or your police intellect? Think about it, Sarah. There's been three murders that we know of. Does he have an alibi for any of them? Do we know where he was? Can anyone confirm his whereabouts or what he was doing? We don't have the answers to those questions, and until we do, we need to consider him as a potential suspect."

"But Lieutenant, he could never do those things. He's not like that."

"Maybe the Nico you know isn't, but what about when he blacks out, like he did tonight? He said he didn't know how he got to this house and the last he remembers is being in front of the diner, then suddenly he finds himself parked in front of the house, which happens to be the scene of a murder."

Sarah heard the truth in Colby's statements and her heart skipped a beat. She knew Nico could never do those horrible things but she also recognized, based on basic police investigative procedures, he could very easily be suspected for these crimes. She looked out the front windshield, tears forming in her eyes, and softly said, "I guess you're right, Lieutenant. What do we do from here?"

"We need to get him down to the station for a formal interview."

"OK. How will you do that?" she asked, dreading the answer.

Colby could see the effect his words were having on her and regretted upsetting her. "Well, I could go by his place with a couple of officers and pick him up, or, preferably, you could bring him down in the morning."

"Me? You want me to arrest him?"

"No, Sarah. Not arrest, just bring him down to the P.D. I told you I consider him a person of interest, not a suspect at this point. I just need to talk with him, get some things cleared up if I can. There is a little too much coincidence here to ignore, in spite of your feelings for him. Can you do that?"

"I suppose so. What time do you want him there?"

"Around 8:30 would be good. Now, I don't want you to tell him about our conversation tonight, OK? Just tell him I have a few questions I need to clear up. Promise?"

"I promise. I'll get him there on time."

"Thanks, Sarah. Oh, and you are not to take part in the interview, understand?"

"I'd like to sit in, Sir. I won't ask any questions or interrupt."

"No, Sarah. You are too close to him and I want him to be out of his comfort zone during our talk. It's the best way to make sure he stays focused, that I'm getting the truth."

Sarah realized the wisdom of Colby's plan. Interrogation success depended on the person being uncomfortable in the surroundings. "All right, Lieutenant. Is that all?"

"Yes, and I am truly sorry for upsetting you."

Sarah didn't answer as she opened the door and got out of the car.

Chapter 17

Nico and Sarah walked into the police department just before 8:30 the next morning. Sarah waved at the clerk and she passed them through the locked hallway door. She led the way to Lieutenant Colby's office, knocked on the jamb and ushered Nico in. "Good morning, Lieutenant," she said as Nico sat down in the chair next to the desk.

"Good morning, Sarah, Nico. Can I offer you some coffee, or tea?"

Sarah said she was good and asked Nico if he wanted anything.

"No, thanks Sarah. Are you staying with us?"

"No, I'm not. Got some reports to catch up on so come find me when you're done." Turning to Lieutenant Colby she said, "I'll be in the conference room if you need me for anything," then turned and left the office, closing the door behind her.

Sarah tried to concentrate on the background of the latest murder victim but found it hard to stay focused. She was worried about Nico and the interview with the Lieutenant. She knew Nico could not be involved in the murders but was anxious that he did not have an alibi. She shook her head and took a couple of deep breaths and turned her attention to the latest victim.

Mary Louise Donaldson was seventy-four years old and suffering from a severe case of chronic obstructive pulmonary disease. She had been a chain smoker for more than fifty years and her lungs had been destroyed. Several prescriptions of corticosteroids and bronchodilators were found in the house, along with a couple of oxygen tanks and a breathing machine. Sarah copied down the doctor's name on the prescriptions and the pharmacy phone number, intending to make a call to them a bit later. She noticed that Mary Louise's doctor worked at the same hospital where Professor Savage had been treated. She didn't think it too unusual, as that was the only hospital in San Donorio, though there were numerous small clinics and doctors' offices. She filed that info away in her head, thinking she would tell Lieutenant Colby later that day.

Sarah spent the next hour writing her report, stopping every few minutes to look at her watch and wondering about Nico and the interview. Two and a half hours had passed since she had brought him in and she was becoming more and more anxious.

Just as she started to get up to check on him, Lieutenant Colby came into the room. He closed the door behind him before sitting at the table.

"How are things going, Sarah? You doing OK?"

"Yes Sir. Been busy running down some info on our latest victim."

"Good, good. We'll get together later and you can fill me in. I wanted to let you know about the interview with Nico."

"Oh, thank you. I've been kind of worried. I hope everything is OK," she said, hopefully.

"It's getting there. Let me tell you where we stand. Nico is currently in one of the interview rooms. He has agreed to stay with us while we check a couple of things out."

"So he's not under arrest?"

"No, he's not." Lieutenant Colby paused for a moment; "Look, Sarah, for what it's worth, I don't think he had anything to do with the murders, but we still haven't been able to establish his alibi. He's been very cooperative and I don't believe he's been untruthful."

"That's good to know, Lieutenant."

"However, we still need to confirm he was where he said he was at the time of the murders. We know he left the campus a little after ten p.m. the night of the murder, which is right around the time the professor was killed. He claims to have been at home, at his apartment during the time of death of Donna Lapin. He said he was with you earlier that evening and that you came over his apartment for coffee after dinner. Said you were together until around eleven p.m. when you left. The time of death for Donna Lapin has been determined to be between one a.m. and three a.m., and Nico has no alibi for that time. The time of death for our latest victim has been set between eleven a.m. and 4 p.m. yesterday. Curiously, Nico has no alibi for that time frame and ends up, somehow, in front of the house, finds the body and reports it to us. Don't you think it odd he didn't call you before going in to say he'd found the house we have been searching for over the last two days."

"It is odd, but it doesn't surprise me he did that. He has some sort of connection with the killer, some mental bond with him and he sees things the killer sees."

"Really? So why is this the first I've heard of it? Didn't you think it important enough to share it with me?"

Oh crap, she thought, *Didn't mean to say that.*

"No, Sir, I mean, no I didn't think it wasn't important."

"So why didn't you tell me?"

"I didn't think you would take me seriously. I didn't believe it when Nico first told me, so I could imagine what you're response would have been."

"You could have a little more faith in me, Sarah. I might not have given it a lot of credence, but I wouldn't have totally ignored it."

Sarah paused a moment, gathering her thoughts, "Can I speak freely, Sir?"

"Of course you can."

"OK. I don't want you to think I'm complaining, but at times you haven't exactly treated me with much respect. You have made me feel like I'm just in the way around here, and sometimes the work you have me doing really isn't what I should be doing."

"What do you mean, Sarah? You've done a good job for us and the work I've assigned you is necessary and important."

"I know, Lieutenant, but it's work that could easily have been handled by a clerk or community service aide. I just feel you are not using me like you should. I should have been out there with the patrol officers, helping them search for the house, looking for witnesses or evidence. I should have a more active role. After all, the first homicide did occur on campus, and I found the body."

Lieutenant Colby thought for a few moments about what she said. He realized she was right. He had been a bit condescending towards her lately, had not taken her seriously.

"I'm so sorry you feel that way, Sarah. I didn't intend to do that and I apologize."

"I know you didn't, Sir, it's just that it was embarrassing in front of the other guys, and thanks. So, what do we do about Nico?"

"I don't really know. I'm going to release him in a bit."

Sarah's face lit up and she smiled, saying "That's good news."

"Well, I'm only doing it because we have no evidence to connect him to the crimes. Can't prove it, but still can't disprove it."

"Can I take him home?" she asked.

"Yeah, but give us about twenty minutes. He's agreed to provide us with a set of elimination prints, so as soon as that's done, he'll be free to go."

"Great, Sir. I'll be in here when he's done, so just let me know and I'll come get him."

"OK. Now, tell me about this supposed connection he has with the killer."

Sarah took the next few minutes to tell him everything she knew about the connection Nico felt with the Sin Eater and how he seemed to be getting more and more visions. She told him she felt it could be a real advantage for them, that they may be able to find the suspect sooner because of it.

"Hmmm, I can see how it could help," Colby mused, "But I need to talk to Nico about this."

"Today?" Sarah asked.

"No, not today," he replied. "Maybe tomorrow or the next day."

"All right. Thanks again, lieutenant, I really do appreciate it."

"You're welcome, Sarah. I know I haven't told you this before, but you are a good cop. You know what you're doing, and you are smart. If you ever want to lateral over to us, you can count on a good recommendation from me."

"Really? That's good to know. Thank you, Sir."

"No problem. Well, back to work," Colby said, smiling as he turned and left the room.

Chapter 18

Sarah dropped Nico off at his apartment with the promise that he not do anything about his visions without contacting her first. They made plans for dinner at her place later that afternoon. Sarah told him to stay home and rest for a couple of hours and to meet her at her apartment at four. She told him she needed to go back to the department to finish up some paperwork and wouldn't get home until after three.

Nico smiled at her and said, "You sound like my mother."

"Well, I've never met her but if that's the case, I like her already!" She took his hand and kissed him on the cheek. "Seriously, just take it easy and meet me at my place later, OK?"

"OK. See you at four.

After Sarah left Nico made himself a cup of tea and retreated to the living room couch. He read the front page of the newspaper and drank the tea. He found himself getting drowsy and lay down on the couch, thinking he would take a little nap. Setting his watch alarm for two hours, he dozed off into a dreamless sleep.

Sarah left the police department at three and stopped at the market to pick up a few things on the way home. As she walked back to her car carrying the two bags of groceries she didn't notice the man walking twenty feet behind her. She placed one of the bags on the ground next to her car and fished her keys out of her pocket. As she unlocked the door, Jacob came up behind her and struck her on the temple with a sock tightly packed with sand, a homemade blackjack designed to render the victim unconscious without causing serious injury. Sarah dropped like a stone and as she fell, he caught her and eased her into the front seat of her car. He picked up the keys she had dropped on the ground and looked around, seeing no one in the parking lot that would have seen what he had done. He climbed into the driver's seat, pushing Sarah to the passenger side, closed the door, started the car and drove off.

***

The beeping of his watch awoke him and he got up, stretching the kinks from his muscles. Looking at his watch and saw it was nearly three o'clock as he made his way into the bathroom to get ready for their dinner date. After he had showered, shaved and dressed, he left to meet Sarah, stopping along the way at the local Safeway to buy some flowers. He was looking forward to this evening and the chance to just relax with her and to forget about things for a while.

Nico had grown very fond of Sarah. Some of his best time was spent with her as he enjoyed her company and found her charming and intelligent. He was falling in love with her and knew it. She made him happy.

Parking in front of her building Nico walked up the stairs to her door. He knocked and waited a bit, then knocked again and called out her name. Still receiving no answer, he thought she might be in the shower and didn't hear him, so he went back to his car and leaned up against it to wait a few minutes.

After fifteen minutes, he looked up at her apartment window. There seemed to be a dark mist in the air, and he got the feeling that Sarah was in danger. He looked around wildly, seeing nothing that could be a threat, but the feeling wouldn't go away. Nico became alarmed, dropped the flowers and ran up the stairs to her door. He knocked on the door saying loudly, "Sarah? Are you in there?" Not hearing a reply, nor the sound of anyone coming to the door, he knocked again, louder this time, again calling out her name. After ten seconds, he tried the door knob and found it unlocked.

He opened the door and stepped inside while calling out to her. A quick search of the apartment and revealed it was empty. The feeling of evil was so strong that he knew the Sin Eater had been here and that Sarah was in grave danger. The apartment had not been ransacked and nothing seemed to be disturbed, and there was no sign of forced entry or a struggle. Standing in the small living room and looking around he spotted a neatly folded sheet of note paper leaning on a decorative bowl on the counter separating the kitchen from the living room. Walking over and picking it up, he saw his name written on it. While holding it he immediately felt a burning sensation in his hand that shot up his arm. Nico dropped the paper and grabbed his arm as the feeling faded almost immediately. Shocked by the effect of touching something the Sin Eater had handled, he hesitated a moment before reaching down to retrieve the note. He extended his hand and barely touched it and again felt a surge of evil in his fingers, like an electric shock. Closing his eyes and taking a deep breath, he felt something come over him, something that calmed him, that cleared his head, a feeling of power. After a half a minute, he felt stronger and picked it up. He no longer felt the burning sensation, just a tingling in his hand, and was able to unfold it. There was a short printed note on it.

I have your girlfriend. Come alone to the old fruit warehouse at 1625 Third St. Do not notify the police. Do not make me hurt her.

Shocked, Nico re-read the note, then sat down on one of the stools at the counter. He read the note one more time, then dropped it. His heart was beating rapidly and he was starting to hyperventilate. He took several deep breaths to calm himself and clear his head. After a couple of minutes, he knew what he had to do. Getting up he calmly walked out of the apartment, closing the door behind him, and headed to his car.

Consciousness returned slowly to Sarah. The first thing she became aware of was that she was sitting in a wooden chair and she couldn't move her arms or legs. She was aware of a musty smell as if something wet and moldy lay nearby. She opened her eyes and looked around, seeing she was alone in a large room. There were empty wooden shelves and racks along both walls and closed metal rollup doors at each end. Along the top of each wall were rows of dirty windows, some broken, letting in enough light so she could see she was alone. Sarah realized there was duct tape across her mouth, keeping her from calling out or shouting and her arms were duct taped to the arms of the chair. Her legs were taped to the chair legs, effectively keeping her from moving. She could see she was sitting in the center of the building. There were large cardboard boxes scattered in one corner of the room, and all was quiet.

Sarah felt dizzy and had a throbbing headache. Her head hurt and she could feel blood on her temple and cheek. She remembered opening her car door in the grocery lot, then a sharp pain to her temple. Fireworks went off behind her eyes, followed by darkness as consciousness left her. She had not seen the person who attacked her, but she strongly suspected their murder suspect was responsible. She didn't understand why she was held here in this dank place, why she wasn't dead.

We must have been getting too close to finding him, she thought, *But why take me captive? What purpose...* and then it hit her. *NICO!! He's using me to get Nico here.*

Sarah shook her head and rotated it, stretching her neck, trying to clear her head. She could feel the blood on her head and cheek was still tacky, not completely dry. Since it hadn't dried, she guessed she had been out for no more than fifteen or twenty minutes. That would mean she must be within ten minutes of the grocery store and her apartment, and by the look of the building, it must be in the old warehouse district near the train tracks. Being familiar with the area she knew the warehouses were mostly abandoned and the area deserted, except for some homeless squatters.

Once her head had cleared and the dizziness passed, she started looking more carefully at her bindings. Several wraps of duct tape bound her wrists tightly to the chair. She struggled against the tape but was unable to loosen her wrists. She tried to pull her ankles loose from the chair legs with the same result. She screamed behind the tape over her mouth, the tape muffling the sound, tears of frustration running down her cheeks.

Sarah tried to scoot the chair across the floor, or at least tip it over, but was again frustrated when she realized it was bolted to the floor. She screamed again and again, struggling against her bindings until she became exhausted and her throat raw. She sat limply in the chair, her chin resting on her chest, and cried softly.

***

Nico sat in his car parked in front of Sarah's apartment. He took out his cell phone and dialed a number.

"Hi, Ma, how's it going?"

"Hello Nico. I've been expecting your call."

Nico was not surprised at this; "There's something I need to talk to you about."

"I know, honey, and I think I can help. Tell me all about it."

It took him ten minutes to tell her everything, including his latest visions that led him to the murder house the previous day.

"So, I'm going after her, Ma, without the police."

"Is that a good idea, son? Just you, alone?"

"Probably not, but I don't see any other alternative."

"What will you do once you get there?"

"I don't know, but I'll figure it out when I get there. Look, Ma, I don't know how this is going to end and if it ends badly, know that I love you and you have been the most important person in my life. I want you to know..."

"Stop right there, Nico!" she blurted. "You need to stop thinking like that. This will turn out ok if you concentrate and use the gifts you have to your advantage."

"What are you talking about, Ma?"

"Honey, you have these visions for a reason. Do you remember what I told you last week about our name, Guardino, that in Italian it means guardian?"

"Yeah, what about it?"

"We are called that for a reason, a reason that goes back centuries."

"I remember, too, that you said that I have these visions for a reason. Are they connected?"

"I had hoped to never have this conversation with you, Nico, but apparently it has been forced upon us. It seems we can't escape our heritage, honey."

"I don't have a lot of time, Ma, so please, tell me what I need to know."

"OK, son. Keep an open mind, and don't interrupt until I am done."

Chapter 19

S arah didn't know how long she had been sitting alone in the warehouse. She started working loose the tape covering her mouth by moving her jaw around and by using her tongue to wet the tape, little by little. After several minutes she had loosened it enough that she was able to slowly roll it up by rubbing her jaw and mouth along her shoulders. After a few more minutes, she was able to pull one side away, clearing her mouth. She was thankful that the Sin Eater had not wrapped the tape completely around her head.

She worked her jaw and licked her chapped lips. After a few minutes she leaned over to see if she could get her teeth on the tape holding her wrist to the chair and found she could just stretch enough. She began by again wetting the tape at the edge and biting at it until she was able to lift one edge slightly. It took her nearly fifteen minutes to make that much progress, the effort making the sweat run down her forehead. She stopped and rested for a few minutes, breathing deeply, before she started again on the loosened edge.

Sarah renewed her efforts as she began to worry about how much time had passed. There was no telling when the Sin Eater would return and she wanted to get free before that happened.

After another ten minutes one side of the tape came up a little, but since there were several wraps around her wrist and the arm of the chair, it was too strong for her to tear. Stopping to rest again she began to sob softly in frustration. She leaned back in the chair to rest her aching neck and shoulders and closed her eyes.

A noise from the end of the warehouse near the small entrance door by the roll-up caught her attention. Her heart was beating wildly as she held her breath, hoping it was just the wind rattling it. The door slowly opened a few inches, letting in a beam of light. Suddenly a shadow blocked the light, and she gasped as the door started to swing further inward.

***

Nico listened without interrupting while his mother spoke, becoming more and more incredulous at what she was telling him.

"That's why you have this connection with him, Nico. It's been that way for generations in our family. We have been tasked with preventing evil from flourishing, stopping it whenever we can, by any means we can. You have the means and the power to stop this evil, Nico."

"How do I do that, Ma?" he asked.

"Let yourself go, Nico. Just let yourself go. Clear your mind, let the power emerge. It's already inside of you, a part of you. You can control it, Nico. You just have to let it grow."

Nico thought about it for a few moments, muttering, "Just let it grow."

Nico said into the phone, "Look, Ma, I gotta get going. Sarah is in trouble and needs me. I'll call you back in a while. I love you."

"Be careful, Honey. I love you too."

Nico disconnected the call and started the car. He took a deep breath, put the car in drive, and pulled away from the curb heading to the warehouse while the things his mother told him a few minutes earlier bounced around his head. Up till now he had no idea he was endowed with this power and that he, and generations of his ancestors, were tasked with combating evil.

It now made sense why he had a connection to the Sin Eater. He felt better now that he knew these things. Knowledge was power.

***

Sarah held her breath as the door swung open. Someone outside stepped into the dimly lit room, silhouetted in the doorway

"What do you want?" she yelled, struggling against her bonds. "Let me go. I'm a police officer. You don't want to make this any worse."

"Sarah?"

She stopped struggling, surprised at the voice. "Nico? Is that you?"

Nico stepped further into the warehouse, seeing her in the chair as his eyes adjusted to the dim light. "Yes, Sarah. Are you OK?"

"I'm fine, Nico. He's tied me to the chair. I can't get loose."

"Are you alone?"

"I think so. I've been here for about an hour. Haven't seen him or heard from him."

Nico ran over to the chair and knelt in front of her. He gently pulled the tape from her face. Seeing the blood on the side of her head he said, "You're bleeding! What happened?"

"He clubbed me when I wasn't looking. I was at the supermarket and was loading my groceries in the car when he hit me. Next thing I knew I was taped to this chair in the middle of the warehouse."

"Did you see him, talk to him?"

"No, I was alone when I woke up. Been trying to get loose ever since."

"I'll have you out of here in a couple of minutes," Nico said as he worked at loosening the tape around her wrists.

As Nico worked on the tape he felt something inside him, a warmth, slowly becoming more and more intense until it seemed to spread to his entire body. He felt his head clearing, the fears he had been feeling fade. A new strength was coursing through him and suddenly it became clear to him what he had to do. As he freed Sarah he couldn't help but smile to himself.

Jacob was watching the warehouse from behind a pile of boxes against the next warehouse. He saw Nico arrive and enter the building where he had put the woman. He had placed the note under the wiper blade of Nico's car when he first went inside, hoping this would scare them both into abandoning their search for him.

He watched as Nico lead the girl cop out, stopping by the door to look around, his gaze lingering on the pile of boxes as if he knew Jacob was watching them. Jacob frowned when he saw Nico smile. A shudder rippled through him as they turned and walked to the car.

Nico opened the door for Sarah and helped her into the passenger seat, saying, "I'm taking you to the hospital, Sarah. You need to get your head looked at."

"No, Nico, I'm fine. Take me to the police department. I need to talk to Inspector Colby."

"No, you may need stitches and there's a good chance you've sustained a concussion. You need to be looked at by a doctor." Nico handed her his cell phone. "Call him, have him meet you there, OK?"

"But..."

"But nothing. Don't argue. Call him and tell him to meet us at the hospital."

Sarah grinned at him and said, as she dialed the phone, "I do have a pretty good headache. OK, Nico, to the hospital we go."

Nico started the car and drove out of the area, pulling over a couple of blocks away. He pulled the note he found under the wiper and held it up, saying "Found this on the windshield. I'd bet he put it there after I arrived."

"What's it say?"

"Don't know. Haven't read it yet. I wanted to get you out of danger area first." Nico unfolded the note, and began reading it out loud. "Let this serve as a warning, Guardian, to you and the woman cop. If I had wanted to really hurt her, I could have. I chose not to.

"Leave me be. I have God's work to do and I will allow nothing, and no one, to interfere with it. If you don't back off, the next time I won't be so merciful to her, or you. This is your only warning."

"So this whole thing was meant as a warning? Does he really believe we would stop the investigation? He couldn't possibly think this would work, could he?"

"I think he does, Sarah. Remember, we are not dealing with a rational man here. He's a psychotic killer who believes he is doing the Lord's work. He has righteous indignation in his mind. Who are we to interfere with his calling?" Nico paused for a few moments, then turned to Sarah and said, "By the way, I know he was there, at the warehouse, watching us as we left."

"Oh my God!" she exclaimed. "I didn't see him anywhere around. Where was he?"

"Standing behind a pile of boxes by the next warehouse."

"Did you see him?"

"No, but I could feel his presence. I'm tuned into him, remember? And, I know his name. It's Jacob Sondimere."

"Do you know where he is now?"

Nico paused a moment before answering. He realized if he concentrated on him, he could "see" where Jacob was, what he was doing. Even now, he could see him as he walked past the warehouses and turned towards the downtown area. He recognized buildings as the Sin Eater passed them, could feel what he was feeling, could almost know what he was thinking. In spite of this, he told Sarah "No, not now. I think we have to be closer to each other before I connect to him."

Sarah turned to him, stating, "You know Lieutenant Colby has been checking on your whereabouts when the murders were committed. He told me you are considered a person of interest since there is no one who can vouch for your actions or location during the time frames of the killings."

"So he thinks of me as a suspect?"

"No, Nico, not a suspect. A person of interest. It's different. He also told me he doesn't believe you were involved, but he would not be doing his job if he didn't cover all angles."

"Yes, I can understand that." He looked at her and smiled; "I'm not worried about it."

Sarah smiled back at him and stated, "I'm not either."

They rode in silence the rest of the way, each concerned by their own thoughts, until Nico pulled into the hospital parking lot.

Nico and Sarah arrived at the small emergency clinic a mile or so from the hospital before the police or Lieutenant Colby arrived, so she used the lag time to register. A nurse came out and looked at her injury, made some notes on her chart, then told one of the nursing assistants to get a cold pack and a gauze pad for her head. She told Sarah to have a seat, that a doctor would see her in a little while.

After waiting a few minutes, Lieutenant Colby and two officers entered the emergency room. Spotting Sarah and Nico, they walked directly over to them.

"You OK, Sarah?" Colby asked. "Have you been seen by a doctor?"

"I'm all right, Lieutenant. Just a bit of a headache. The Sin Eater abducted me. Hit me on the head and took me to a warehouse. He tied me to a chair and gagged me and left me alone."

"How'd you get away?" he asked, sitting next to her.

"Actually, I had managed to get partially loose when Nico showed up and got me out of there." She looked at Nico and smiled. "He's got more info for you, LT. He said he was left a couple of notes."

"Is that right, Nico?"

"Yes, Sir. I found one at Sarah's apartment and another on my windshield when we escaped from the warehouse."

"Do you have them with you?"

"I have the second one," he replied, pulling it from his pocket and handing it to Lieutenant Colby. Colby grabbed it very gingerly by a corner using his thumb and forefinger and asked one of the officers to get him an envelope for the note. "The first one is still at Sarah's apartment and there was a warning in it and the address where she was being held."

"Hmm, that's odd!" Colby exclaimed. "Anyone else but you handle the notes, Nico?" Colby asked.

"No, Sir, at least as far as I know."

"OK, that's good. Maybe, with a little luck, we'll finally get this guy's prints."

Nico stood up as a doctor approached them and watched as he checked Sarah's injury. "Not too bad, Miss. Gonna need four or five stitches and I'll want to do a couple of tests to see if you have a concussion, but barring that, you should be fine in a few days. Come with me and we'll get you fixed up."

"How long will this take, Doctor?" Nico asked.

"Oh, I'd say a couple of hours. Longer if she shows signs of a concussion."

Turning to Sarah he took her in his arms and hugged her and kissed her on the forehead. "There's something I need to attend to, but I'll be back as quick as I can. If I don't get back in time, maybe the Lieutenant can give you a ride home and I'll meet you there later, OK?

"What are you up to, Nico?" Sarah asked, grabbing his hand.

"Just a little personal business. I'll be back as soon as I can." Nico turned to Colby and asked, "Is that OK with you, Lieutenant?"

"Yeah, it's OK. I'm gonna need your statement, but it can wait a couple of hours. I'll be here until she's released, and I'll make sure she gets home safely. There will be an officer posted out front of her place until we catch this guy. Go take care of what you need to."

"Thank you, Lieutenant." Nico smiled at Sarah, turned and headed toward the door.

"Nico," Sarah called out, "Be careful and don't do anything foolish."

Chapter 20

Jacob Sondimere walked through the downtown area, headed toward his hotel when he again felt as if someone was watching him. He stopped and looked around, seeing no one unusual. He hadn't figured out why he felt that way, what was causing his uneasiness, but he knew what needed to be done. There was another client that needed his help, who had to be cleansed and have his path to heaven cleared. The sooner the better, he thought.

He had found a potential client in the hospital's files two nights ago, a man, Frank Johnson, suffering from terminal pancreatic cancer. His weight loss had been listed as "severe" and the prognosis was not good. The doctors had given him less than two months to live and had prescribed morphine to help manage the pain he was suffering. According to his hospital records he lived alone, cared for by an LVN from eight a.m. until eight p.m. when he would retire for the night. The next of kin was listed as a son who lived in Oregon, and there were plans to move him to a hospice care center next week.

It was the only thing that would calm Jacob, though the nausea and shakes he endured after completing a ceremony made it a difficult recovery. He was rapidly approaching the point where he would start suffering from the headaches that always plagued him when he let too much time pass between servicing clients. This diversion with the Guardian cost him more than two days, and he could feel the pressure building inside his head.

He was not worried about the Guardian again interfering with his work. Jacob knew Nico was involved emotionally with the woman cop, and, in his naivety, felt he had made it clear to him to stay away, that he had instilled enough fear for her safety so he would back off. With these thoughts, he entered his room to shower, shave and put on his clean suit.

Nico drove out of the hospital parking lot and two blocks down the road pulled into a strip mall parking lot. He parked near the street, away from the shops and turned off the engine. He closed his eyes, cleared his mind and concentrated on connecting with the Sin Eater, letting the power take hold of him.

At first nothing came to him other than a faint sound he couldn't identify. After a few moments, it became a bit louder and he had a blurry vision of running water. After another minute, he realized it was the sound of a shower and could clearly see the water cascading down from the showerhead. Nico realized he was hearing and seeing what the Sin Eater heard and saw while he was taking a shower. He cleared the image and sound from his mind to try to learn where the Sin Eater was without success. All he could get was a name, Frank, and a feeling of anticipation, purpose, and excitement. Nico could feel the Sin Eater was planning to murder another person, and soon, but nothing else came to him.

Nico took a few deep breaths and concentrated harder, seeking to get into the Sin Eater's mind, find out more about Frank. One thing he was certain of was that Frank would be the next victim. As flashes of thoughts flew through his mind, one recurring sight was of a folder, possibly containing a record of some sort, and another was of an empty hallway, dimly lit, with evenly spaced doors on each side.

Nico knew he had seen the hallway before, had been there, but couldn't quite place where it was. He had the feeling the records folder and hallway were important to the Sin Eater, but in what way he didn't know. Not yet anyway.

He shook his head, clearing it, closed his eyes and tried again to connect with him, and after a few moments began to get a picture of a house with an overgrow lawn, an ordinary looking home. It was somewhat run down and painted a faded white with peeling dark brown trim. He could see the front of the house and as he watched he saw a woman come out the front door, walk down the porch, and get into a cab waiting at the curb. As it drove away, he envisioned walking toward the front porch and up to the front door. He paused before entering and looked around, scanning the street in both directions. He saw other houses and some stores down the block. The vision ended and Nico opened his eyes, gasping.

I know where this is! He thought. With a flash of recognition, Nico knew it was Frank's house and, more importantly, knew he was seeing what would happen later today. He smiled to himself and took out his cell phone.

Sarah was sitting on an exam table in the treatment after receiving six stitches to her head, waiting for a nurse to take her to the neurology room when her phone rang. She took her phone from her pocket and saw the call was from Nico.

"Hey, Nico. What's up?"

"I know about the next murder, Sarah."

"What? How?"

"I've seen where he will be going, and who he is going after. I've connected with him, looked through his eyes, gathered his thoughts. I saw a file folder of some sort, and a long, dim hallway with doors on both sides. I've seen that hallway before, Sarah, but I can't remember where. I know he is after someone named Frank, and I know it's important to the case."

"When is this happening, Nico, and where?"

"Later this evening, but I can't tell you where."

"I thought you said you knew where. How do you know it hasn't happened yet? Nico what's going on?"

"I just know it hasn't happened yet, and I do know where. But if I tell you, you will show up with the other police. I can't let that happen. I have to do this on my own."

"Why, Nico? You've got to let me help. This is too dangerous for you."

"I'm sorry, Sarah, it's what I have to do. There is more than one life at stake here. If the police show up, one life may be saved, but another life will perish. I can't let that happen. This has to end once and for all. Whatever happens, Sarah, know that I love you," Nico said and disconnected the call.

"Nico, wait. Please," she begged into the dead phone, her voice shaking with dread. "Nico" she half whispered, the tears filling her eyes.

Nico tossed the phone onto the passenger seat after turning it off. He started the car and began driving, not thinking about where he was going, making turns that he knew were the right ones. It was as if he was driving on autopilot.

As he drove flashes of visions came to him. It was clear the Sin Eater was on the move, walking from his room through a section of town Nico recognized. He knew he was on his way, that their meeting was destined to happen. It was inevitable they would have this final showdown.

Chapter 21

J acob walked down the street, a slight smile on his face. For some reason he felt better, almost happy, knowing he would be helping another client soon. He breathed deeply, and walked briskly.

He suddenly realized that this was the first time in the last week or so that he didn't feel like he was being watched or followed. It was a relief to not have that hanging over him. He felt safe, free of the presence that seemed to be dogging him. He smiled a bit more and hummed softly to himself as he picked up his pace.

Jacob walked up to the house and directly onto the front porch. He tried the front door knob and found it unlocked. Turning it slowly and quietly, he cautiously opened the door and stepped in the darkened room. Closing the door he stood still for a bit, letting his eyes adjust to the shadows.

The house was quiet. He couldn't hear anyone moving around the house, or talking, or the sounds of someone in the kitchen, none of the normal sounds he expected to hear. He knew it was too early for the care worker to have left and wondered where she was. If she was here, he, regretfully, would have to kill her, too. Frank should be here too, getting ready for dinner. It concerned him that all was not as he expected, but he didn't feel there was a threat in the house or anywhere nearby. He remained still and quiet for another minute then began slowly making his way through the house, looking for Frank or the care worker.

***

As soon as Nico disconnected, Sarah wiped the tears from her eyes and left the treatment room and rushed to the waiting room. She ran up to Lieutenant Colby and said, "Nico knows when and where the next murder will be."

"What? Did he call you?"

"Yes, just now. He said he knows."

"Where is he?"

"I don't know. He wouldn't say. He just said it was something he needed to do. He didn't want us involved."

"Did he say anything that could help us find out where he is?"

"He mentioned something about a file folder and a long, dim hallway. He said he had seen it before, and you know what? It seems familiar to me, too."

"We need to follow up on that. Think Sarah, where could that hallway be?"

"I don't know, Sir. Give me a few minutes, maybe I can come up with it."

"OK. Go back to the exam room and try to remember. I'll be out here making a few calls. Maybe he meant the police department? It does match that description."

"Could be, Sir, but that doesn't seem right to me."

"Well, I'll make a few calls while you get fixed up. Come get me if you remember."

"Yes, Sir," Sarah replied. She walked back to the exam room and sat on the table.

I'm missing something, she thought. *If it's familiar to Nico and me, we might have been together when we saw it. God, we've been everywhere together lately. Where can it be? He said the victim's name is Frank and there was a vision of a file. Could it be the file is about Frank? Maybe Colby is right, maybe it's from the police department.*

There's got to be a link between the murders. If I can find that, I'll know what all this means. Let's see, she thought, *Professor Savage was the first and we know he was terminally ill with cancer. Donna Lapin was connected to the professor, but wasn't sick, and then there was Mary Louise Donaldson, who was sick, but not terminal.*

Sarah heard a soft knock on the door and then the doctor entered. "Ready for this, Sarah?" he asked.

"Yep! Let's do it."

"All right, then." He gently probed her wound with a gloved finger. "Has it numbed up?"

"Yeah, I didn't feel a thing."

"OK. This should take just a few minutes."

Sarah's mind went back to her problem of finding a connection between the murders as he started stitching her up. Professor Savage: terminally ill.

Donna Lapin: Listed as the Professor's next of kin, in good health. Mary Louise Donaldson: No connection to Savage or Lapin, not in good health but not terminal. There HAS to be a reason why they were chosen!

Sarah racked her brain trying to put the pieces together. It was almost there, just on the edge of her memory, yet the pieces still eluded her.

"OK, Sarah, all done," the doctor said. "I'll cover it with a loose bandage. I want you to take it easy for the next day or so, even though the tests showed no symptoms of a concussion. You can take the bandage off tomorrow."

"OK, Doc. Thanks. Is it gonna leave a scar?"

"Maybe a thin one, but it should be mostly covered by your hair. Shouldn't be visible."

"Good. Can I go now?"

"Hold on a second. Gotta update your chart."

Sarah watched him as he reached over to the counter and picked up a brown folder, opened it, and began writing. Watching him write, it suddenly came to her.

It's a medical chart! That's what Nico saw, that's why it seemed so familiar to me. If I'm right, then the hallway has to be at the hospital.

Sarah hopped down from the exam table and ran from the room, watched by the surprised doctor.

"Lieutenant," she yelled, "I figured it out!"

"Great, Sarah. So, what's it all about?"

"I'm certain the folder Nico saw was from the hospital. It was a medical file, and the hallway was the one at the hospital Nico and I saw when we went there to talk to the nurses and doctor. That's the connection, Sir."

"It makes sense, Sarah. Savage was dying, and Lapin was listed as his next of kin. Donaldson was pretty sick, and I'll bet she was treated at the hospital. Now we have this next victim, Frank. He has to be a patient there, too."

"I agree. We need to get to the hospital and find out who Frank is, and where he lives. That should lead us to where Nico is, and hopefully, the Sin Eater, too."

"We need to get going, then. Let's hope we figure this out before those two meet."

They dashed out to the parking lot and piled in the Lieutenant's car. He started it up and squealed the tires out of the lot, flipping on the lights and siren as they hit the street.

***

Nico sat quietly in a chair in Frank's darkened bedroom. He had arrived almost forty-five minutes earlier and had managed to convince Frank's care worker that his life was in danger, and hers, too, and they needed to leave right away. She quickly grabbed a few articles of clothing for Frank and his medicine and helped him to her car. She had Nico's credit card and instructions from him to go to the Motel Six a few blocks away and get a room. He told her to stay in the room until he came for her in an hour or two.

As he waited, he felt a calm come over him. His senses sharpened. His hearing was acute, his sense of smell heightened. He could see through the shadows and was able to see the house as if it was half-dark, like dusk. He breathed deeply and set his mind on the Sin Eater. Closing his eyes, he almost immediately saw the front door of Frank's house and a hand reaching for the doorknob. He saw the door opening slowly and could hear the slight squeak of the hinges. A few moments later he heard the latch close softly, and felt a change in the atmosphere in the house, like the slight disturbance of the air when someone walks by you. There was a pervasive evil in the air and it started getting harder to breathe. What he sensed was almost overwhelming, yet he knew he was strong enough to fight it. He took a couple of deep breaths and the sense of dread he felt lessened.

Nico knew the Sin Eater was in the house. The time had come for them to meet, to end this once and for all.

Chapter 22

Sarah and Lieutenant Colby took the elevator to the fourth floor and ran to the nurse's station. The duty nurse looked up as they approached. Recognizing Sarah, she smiled and said, "Hey, Officer, how are you doing?"

Slightly out of breath, Saran replied, "Good to see you again, Nurse. We have an emergency and need your help."

"Oh, my, is someone hurt? Are you two OK?"

"Yes, we're fine, but we need some information that very likely will save lives tonight."

"What kind of information?" she asked.

Sarah passed along the info she had gotten from Nico, without telling her how she had gotten it. The duty nurse was not overly receptive to her request, saying she didn't have the authority to release that kind of confidential information.

"Look, I understand all that," Sarah conceded, lowering her voice, "but you've got to understand how critical this is. People will die if we don't get it, and quickly. This information could lead us to the next possible victim in time to prevent his death. That's the only reason we need it, to stop a man who has killed three people in the last couple of weeks. He won't stop until we catch him, so please, please tell us what we need to know."

The nurse heard the sincerity in her voice, could see the concern in her eyes, and her resolve crumbled.

"OK, but I never told you this, understood?"

"Of course," both Sarah and Lieutenant Colby agreed simultaneously.

"I know we have had a patient here named Frank, Frank Johnson. He's being treated for pancreatic cancer. He's approaching the final stages and the doctor doesn't hold out much hope that further treatment will work."

Sarah looked at Lieutenant Colby and said, "That fits. That's the connection with the other victims. What's his address?"

"It will take me a minute to access that info."

"Please hurry," Sarah urged.

"I'll be right back. I've got to go to the records room. It's just down the hallway. I'll be back as quick as I can."

***

Nico waited patiently. He could hear the soft footsteps of the Sin Eater as he searched the house, going room to room. As his steps came closer to the bedroom, Nico stood up, remaining in the shadows. Nico saw the door knob turning and the door opening. A figure stepped into the room and suddenly stopped, sensing Nico's presence.

"So, you are here," Jacob said. "I didn't sense you until now."

"I've been waiting for you," Nico answered. "You know why I am here."

"To stop me, yes. And you must know I can't let you do that."

"What you are doing is wrong, Jacob," Nico said. He realized he had called him by his first name, but didn't know how he knew it. "The people you are killing don't deserve it, nor do they need it."

"It's what I do, Guardian. I have to clear the way for them, help them along so they can arrive without sin."

"But two of them weren't ready. It wasn't their time. They had no need of your services. They should still be alive."

"It was necessary to take them. They would have interfered with my work, with my helping the others."

"There is no one here for you tonight. He is safe and out of your reach."

Jacob paused for a moment, sensing something familiar in Nico. "I know you," he said, "We have met before, a long time ago."

"Yes. You came when my grandfather was dying. I was just a boy and you terrified me. I never knew why until just few days ago."

"We connected then, but you didn't realize it. The feeling frightened you."

"I'm not frightened any more, Jacob. SO, where do we go from here?"

Jacob didn't answer for a few seconds. He looked around the room. "Are the police on the way?"

"I think so. They should be here in a couple of minutes."

"If that's the case, I will leave you now, Guardian. We will have to settle this another time." Jacob started backing toward the bedroom door.

Nico stood up. "I can't let you do that, Jacob. You need to stay here and surrender to the authorities when they arrive."

"I can't do that."

"And I can't let you leave."

"Then let's finish this," Jacob said, and charged at Nico.

Jacob was thirty years older than Nico and bigger, having a couple of inches in height and twenty-five pounds on him, but Nico was stronger. His youth was an advantage, and he knew how dangerous Jacob could be. Jacob, on the other hand, did not really recognize the full extent of the threat Nico presented.

Jacob lowered his shoulder and crashed into Nico, knocking him backward into the wall. Nico felt the breath leave him as Jacob's shoulder impacted his chest and his head struck the wall behind him. Stars exploded behind his eyes and his knees buckled. He managed to stay on his feet by grabbing the front of Jacob's jacket, struggling to regain his breath and balance. He pushed back and managed to get Jacob off his chest, allowing him to take a deep breath.

From the moment of their first physical contact, Jacob felt the power in Nico. At that point he realized the danger he was in and re-doubled his efforts. He reached out with both hands, grabbed Nico around the neck and squeezed. He put as much pressure as he could on Nico's windpipe, trying to cut off his air. He knew he had to take control of him as quickly as possible, kill him as quickly as he could, and put maximum effort to that end.

Nico felt Jacob's hands around his throat and took another deep breath before the pressure cut off his breathing. He let go of Jacob's coat and grabbed his wrists, trying to pull the hands from his throat. They struggled at this for the next half a minute, until Nico began to struggle for oxygen. His vision began to blur as he tried to breathe, becoming weaker by the moment.

***

Sarah and Colby ran to the car, having gotten the address for Frank Johnson. As they ran, Lieutenant Colby took out his cell and pressed the speed dial for the police department.

"This is Colby. We've found the address where we believe Nico Guardino is and where the suspect is headed. I need units to get there ASAP. Have them set up a perimeter a half a block around the residence. Tell them to keep a low profile, no lights or siren, and do not move in until they hear from me. I should be there in less than five minutes."

Sarah and Colby jumped into Colby's dark blue Crown Vic and Colby pealed out of the lot, turning on his lights and siren. He accelerated quickly and maintained his speed, hitting seventy in the thirty-five mph zone. Weaving in and out of traffic, he blew through the green lights without slowing. As he approached a red light, he braked hard as he got close, cleared it visually to the left and right, then planted the gas to the floor, rocketing through to the other side. He twisted the wheel hard to the right when a UPS truck pulled into his lane, barely missing him. Cranking the wheel hard back to the left he managed to keep the big sedan from spinning out of control.

Sarah hung on for dear life as the weight shift threw her from side to side. The seatbelt lock tightened and helped keep her stable in her seat. She held onto the belt with both hands and helped Colby clear the road by warning him of possible obstacles.

Colby slid around each corner as fast as he could, counter steering to keep him from losing control of the big sedan. Though the ride took only four minutes, Sarah felt like it was taking forever.

Colby shut off the siren when they were five blocks away, then the lights as they got with two blocks. Slowing the car, he pulled to a stop three houses down from their destination. He grabbed his portable radio as they got out of the car and began quickly walking toward the house. Both he and Sarah drew their pistols during their approach. Stopping one house away and out of sight of anyone in Johnson's house, he keyed the radio and quietly ordered the waiting officers to move up.

***

As the blackness started creeping in at the edges of his vision, Nico heard his mother's voice. "Nico, take heart my son, I am with you. Reach out, Nico, reach out to him. Let the power fill you, reach out to him."

Nico stretched out his right hand and placed it on Jacob's forehead. He felt a warmth flow through his arm and out his hand into Jacob's head. The force seemed to gain speed, more and more of it pouring out his hand as if someone had opened a spigot. He felt strength returning to his body and concentrated on the power. He could feel the pure evil in Jacob, pushing back against his hand. He heard a faint screaming from what seemed a long distance away, the sound of many voices crying out in anguish.

The pressure on his throat lessened a bit, allowing air to flow into his lungs. He took several breaths as the pressure continued to ease. His vision cleared and his strength returned. He pushed off the wall and stood up, focusing on Jacob and the power he felt flowing from his hand.

He put his left hand on Jacob's chest, over his heart and felt the power begin to flow from that hand, too. Jacob writhed and twisted against him, trying to break free, but it seemed Nico's hands were welded to his body. Jacob threw his head back and screamed. A blood red fog began pouring from his mouth, rising toward the ceiling and dissipating into the air. Nico watched the fog as it rose toward the ceiling and could see vague shapes swirling through it, twisting and turning as if they were in agony. He could feel their pain and could hear their wailing.

Nico felt the power flowing from him waning the longer he kept in contact with Jacob and after another twenty seconds, the fog stopped coming from Jacob's mouth and he collapsed to the floor, unconscious.

As Nico's hands broke contact, all the strength in his legs left him and he, too collapsed, landing on his hands and knees. He struggled to breathe, gasping for air. His vision was clouded and his hearing muffled and he felt consciousness fading. He saw a shadow enter the room and kneel next to Jacob. Nico heard him talking to Jacob though he couldn't make out the words. After a minute, the figure approached Nico. He placed Nico on his back on the floor and loosened his collar and belt. Nico looked up at him and said, "Jacob?"

"Yes, I am Jacob, just not the Jacob you sought."

"Who, who are you?" he gasped. "You look like him, yet are different."

"I am his son. I have been trying to find him for months."

"Is he alive?"

"Yes, barely. I think he will survive, though he will never fully recover. Whatever happened here emptied him. Are you the Guardian? I have heard about people like you."

"His son? Are you a Sin Eater, too?"

"No. He tried to get me to follow him, take over for him, but it's not what I wanted. I saw what it was doing to him. Each time he completed the ritual, he seemed a bit darker, more morose, changed. Little by little it was taking control of him. He was becoming more and more obsessed until he began finding clients who didn't need his help."

"Why didn't you stop him?"

"I didn't know he was killing people needlessly until he disappeared four years ago. I have spent all my time since then looking for him, searching up and down the valley, checking the local obituaries and newspapers for deaths that could attributed to him. I never could find any that I was certain he was responsible for, at least until I read about the professor's death, then the death of Ms. Lapin.

Nico fought to stay conscious, asking him "How did that make you know it was him?"

"The fact that the professor was terminally ill helped, but when I learned that his friend, Ms. Lapin was murdered the next day, then I knew. I've been following him around town, trying to prevent him from committing any more murders. I stopped him once a few days ago, but I could never find out where he was staying and there never was an opportunity to get him alone. I think he knew I was around, following him. He was always looking around, was very cautious."

"What happens now?" Nico asked, his voice weak.

"Now I collect him and take him home. He is no longer a danger to anyone. All the sins he took from others, all the evil, is gone from him. He's just a shell, a hollow man who will need looking after for the rest of his life."

Nico nodded slowly and closed his eyes. As he lapsed into unconsciousness he heard him say, "Rest now, Guardian. You are done for now. Your friends are on the way as I hear sirens approaching." He stood up and helped his father to his feet, half carrying hem he started for the bedroom door. He stooped and half turned toward Nico, barely conscious. Quietly he said, "Thank you Guardian for freeing him and returning my father to me."

Chapter 23

Nico awoke on a gurney as he was being wheeled into the emergency room. He looked around and saw Lieutenant Colby walking next to him on one side and Sarah walking on the other.

"Did you catch him?" he asked, his voice still weak and raspy.

"Nico? How are you feeling," Sarah asked, taking his hand.

"Tired, thirsty, and I feel like crap," he replied.

"You gave us a scare, Nico. When we stormed the house and found you, I thought you were dead."

"What about Jacob? Did you find him? Is he still alive?"

"He was gone, Nico. You were alone in the house."

Nico thought for a moment, recalling bits and pieces of the events after he collapsed. He vaguely recalled talking to someone about Jacob but his memory was sporadic. He did remember seeing Jacob unconscious on the floor shortly before he lost consciousness, but didn't know if he had survived their encounter.

"He was there, Sarah. We fought and he fell."

"Well, he must have survived. We searched the house and surrounding area without finding him, and none of the officers on the perimeter saw anyone leaving the area."

Lieutenant Colby added, "We were able to lift some prints from one of the notes. They aren't yours or Sarah's so I'm pretty certain they belong to him. We hope to get a print match through our database searches, now that we have a name."

"Will you be going after him, Lieutenant?"

"Yes. We hope to get a warrant issued for his arrest for the murders of Professor Savage, Ms. Lapin, and Mrs. Donaldson. We've got the County Sheriff's heading to his house as we speak. They should be there soon."

They stopped in the emergency room and the ER doctor approached saying, "OK, you two, out, now. We've got a patient to look after. Into the waiting room you go," he said, ushering them toward the door.

Sarah broke off and returned to Nico. Leaning over, she kissed him on the forehead, brushing her hand along his cheek. "I'll be waiting for you, Nico."

Three hours later a nurse pushed Nico, in a wheel chair, out to the waiting room. "He's all yours, Lieutenant."

Sarah asked, "Everything OK, Nurse?"

"Yes, he's fine. No injuries that we can find. Just a bit dehydrated, and suffering from a good case of exhaustion. He'll need to rest and take it easy for the next couple of days."

"I'll make sure he does. Thanks."

Colby wheeled him to her car and helped him into the front seat. Sarah leaned across him to fasten his seat belt, then got in the driver's seat. Rolling her window down she told Lieutenant Colby, "He'll be at my place for a couple of days if you need him. I'll be in tomorrow morning to complete my report, all right?"

"Fine, Sarah. And thanks, Nico, for your help. I'll be in tomorrow early, trying to figure out how I'm going to explain all this to the Chief. You two get some rest. It's been an extraordinary day."

"We will Lieutenant."

On the drive home, Nico told Sarah what he remembered of the events earlier that night.

"I'm pretty sure there was someone else there, Sarah."

"Who could it have been?"

"I don't know. I can't remember, but I get the feeling whoever it was wasn't a threat. I wish I could remember more."

"It's ok, Nico. It's not important. Don't worry about it. I'm sure it will come back to you in time. We'll talk more in the morning."

Nico leaned back in the seat and stared straight ahead, concentrating on the encounter with Jacob. He was quiet the rest of the way to Sarah's.

A half hour later Nico was lying in bed awaiting sleep to overtake him. With his eyes closed, he concentrated on connecting with the Sin Eater, but no matter how much he tried, he couldn't make a connection. He fell into a dreamless sleep a couple of minutes later and slept the sleep of exhaustion for the next ten hours.

He awoke, greatly refreshed, and got up. He could hear Sarah moving about the kitchen and opened the bedroom door. "Good morning, Sarah. Is it ok if I take a shower?"

"Sure, Babe. Make it quick though, breakfast is almost ready."

Nico showered and dressed and made his way to the kitchen.

"So, what else have you found out about Jacob Sondimere?" he asked as he sat at the table.

"Well, we found where he was staying and they executed a search warrant there. Found a couple of medical files from the hospital that he apparently stole. The files were from patients that were ill, some critically, so that's how we believe he chose his victims."

"But how did he get the records? If I remember, access to the records room is strictly limited and controlled?"

"We found out he was employed as a janitor at the hospital. He worked nights there and pretty much had the run of the place. Colby told me they also found some keys at his place and once they found out where he worked, they were able to find one of the keys was to the records room. They compared his key with the hospital keys and it's apparent it's a duplicate. Somehow Jacob was able to get the records room key and have it copied."

"So everything is falling into place now."

"Yes. It seems to be done and over. Only thing left is to find Jacob Sondimere. There's just one thing left that bothers me."

"What's that?" Nico asked.

"I wonder about any other victims of his. It doesn't make sense that ours were his only ones. There has to be others somewhere."

"I would think so, but is there any chance of finding them?"

"I doubt it. We barely have evidence for our own. Colby has contacted the FBI and they are going to look into it, but I don't think they will turn anything up."

"I guess we'll never know."

"Yep. You ready for breakfast?"

"Absolutely. I'm starving!"

"Good. Would you get the newspaper from the hallway first?"

"Sure."

Nico went out the front door to get the paper and found it on the floor next to the entrance. As he stood up with the newspaper and turned toward the door, he saw a piece of notepaper taped to it with the word "Guardian" printed on it. He looked up and down the empty hallway then pulled the paper off the door and went back inside, locking the door after him.

"Sarah, come here a minute. There's something you need to see."

"Can't it wait, Nico? Breakfast is ready."

"No, sorry, it can't."

Something in his voice made her stop what she was doing and make her way to the couch. Sitting next to him she asked, "What is it, Nico?"

He held up the paper and unfolded it. "It's a note, addressed to me. It's signed Jacob Sondimere Junior."

"Who? Jacob Junior?"

Nico paused and thought for a moment. "I remember now," he exclaimed. He turned to Sarah, "Remember I told you of the other person at the house? He was Jacob's son!"

Nico told her about his conversation with him as the memories came spilling into his brain. "He told me he was taking his father away, that he was no longer a danger, no longer the man he used to be."

"Hmmm, he must have helped his father slip through our perimeter. What else does it say?"

"Not much. Just that he is taking his father somewhere safe, somewhere far away so no one will find them. He thanked me for saving his father, and was glad I ignored his note in the diner warning me to back away." Looking up at her he said, "I don't think he will ever be found."

"Do you think he is telling the truth?"

Nico stared at the letter, thinking of what Jacob's son had said at the house. He smiled "I do, Sarah. I really do."

If you enjoyed this author's book, then please place a review up at the site of purchase, and any social media sites you frequent!

You can find ALL our books up on our website at:

https://www.writers-exchange.com

All our mysteries:

https://www.writers-exchange.com/category/genres/mystery-thrillers-suspense/

All John's Books:

https://www.writers-exchange.com/john-schembra/

About the Author

John Schembra was born Jan. 3, 1948 and raised in the San Francisco Bay Area.

He retired Feb. 2001 from a small northern California police department as a Sergeant after almost 30 years' service.

Prior to becoming a police officer, he was a Military Policeman assigned for a year to the 557th MP Co., Long Binh, Bien Hoa, South Vietnam, where he had several "adventures" that provided the basis for his first novel, *MP*.

He has earned a B.A in Administration of Justice and an M.A in Public Administration. He spent his retirement time writing as well as teaching other police officers emergency vehicle operation/pursuit driving through the Contra Costa County Sheriff's Office and Police Academy. He also instructs officers in the driving simulators, is a train the trainer for emergency vehicle/pursuit/ simulator instructors, and has been recognized as a Subject Matter Expert by the State of California in emergency vehicle operations/pursuit driving.

He has had several trade articles published in law enforcement magazines such as *Law and Order*, *Police Officer's Quarterly*, and *The Backup*. He is also a member of the Police Writers Association, a very supportive writers' group for anyone affiliated with any type of law enforcement organization.

In his spare time (what little there is) John enjoys reading, fishing, and most of all, spending time with his family.

John's personal website is: http://www.jschembra.com

You can keep track of John's work on his author website: https://www.writers-exchange.com/John-Schembra/

If you want to read more about other books by this author, they are listed on the following pages...

An Echo of Lies

The prospects for recovery for Officer Bob Kelly were not good. Shot twice during a traffic stop, the emergency room doctors had worked feverishly to save his life. Four weeks later, to the doctor's surprise, Kelly walked out of the hospital and went home. He felt good--no pain, fully alert, and strong. Little did he know the terror and struggle that awaited him as the demon who possessed him took more control.

Publisher: https://www.writers-exchange.com/an-echo-of-lies/

A Vince Torelli Novel

{Historical: Vietnam War}

MP - A Novel of Vietnam (War: Vietnam)

As Vincent Torelli stepped off the plane at Bien Hoa Air Base, South Vietnam, in June 1967, he was almost overwhelmed by the stench in the hot, humid air. Drafted into the armed forces five months earlier, he still can't comprehend how he ended up in this place, now a Military Policeman assigned to the 557th MP Co. at Long Binh Post just outside Bien Hoa City.

His year-long tour of duty in Vietnam changes him from a somewhat naïve young man to a battle-hardened veteran. Through unlucky chance, Vince becomes involved in the ferocious '68 Tet offensive, barely surviving the night. He sees and experiences things he could never have imagined before ending up in Vietnam.

This is Vince's story... survival, coping with the hell he's facing, the sorrow of lives lost, and the friendships he formed.

Publisher: https://www.writers-exchange.com/mp-a-novel-of-vietnam/

A Vince Torelli Mystery

A former soldier who becomes a San Francisco police homicide investigator after the war, Vince Torelli is dedicated, intelligent and highly principled--all skills that serve him well given the difficult, almost impossible murder investigations he's assigned to handle that force him to the razor edge with equally resolute, extremely ruthless masterminds.

Book 1: Retribution (Mystery: Serial Killer)

There's a vigilante killer loose in San Francisco, and when the justice system fails, he doles out his own brand of justice.

Homicide Inspector Vince Torelli has handled some of the city's worst murders, but this case has him baffled. It seems no matter what he does, the killer manages to stay one step ahead of him, anticipating his every move. The false clues and trail the killer leaves keeps Vince chasing shadows as the body count rises. Will he discover the killer's identity and will he survive long enough to bring him to justice?

Publisher: https://www.writers-exchange.com/retribution/

Book 2: Diplomatic Immunity (Mystery/Thriller)

There are sixty-six Consulates and Embassies in San Francisco and a very talented, deadly sniper is targeting the Consul Generals seemingly at random.

San Francisco Homicide inspector Vince Torelli has a reputation for solving the toughest cases in the city, but this one is unlike anything else he has faced. The killings make no sense, lack motive, and appear to be unrelated but Vince knows there has to be a link between them. As he struggles to find the connection and identify the suspect he becomes a target himself. This can end only one of two ways: Either he solves the case...or he becomes a victim himself.

Publisher: https://www.writers-exchange.com/diplomatic-immunity/

Book 3: Blood Debt

San Francisco Homicide Investigator and Vietnam veteran Vince Torelli strives to clean up the violence in San Francisco but, after a suspect in a double murder is killed during an attempted arrest, he finds himself also protecting the police officers of the city he considers family. His efforts put him in the line of fire when he's targeted. The brother of the suspect victim wants revenge on the officers responsible and he'll stop at nothing. He kidnaps Vince, a man obsessively loyal to his job as well as those he works alongside, a man as smart and committed to his principles as the criminals he catches almost without fail. Vince knows best, though, a blood debt always demands payment...

Publisher: https://www.writers-exchange.com/blood-debt/

Book 4: The List

A recently mutilated, naked corpse is found in an early 19th century tunnel under San Francisco. With no forensic evidence, solving the crime seems impossible.

After San Francisco Homicide Inspector Vince Torelli begins investigating, notes from the killer, addressed to him, start showing up. Vince realizes this murder may be the first of several, leading Vince on a deadly multi-state investigation.

Publisher: https://www.writers-exchange.com/the-list/

Book 5: Southern Justness

When his uncle, a Superior Court Judge in Georgia, is killed in a hit-and-run accident, San Francisco PD Homicide Inspector Vince Torelli travels to Augusta for the funeral.

While there, it is discovered the judge's death was no accident, and Vince gets caught up in a deadly vendetta against his family. Unofficially working with Detective Sergeant Louisa "Louie" Princeton, Richmond County Sheriff's Department, several suspects are eventually identified. Louie and Vince are determined to bring them to justice, but someone is frustrating their attempts with deadly results.

Publisher: https://www.writers-exchange.com/southern-justice/

Sin Eater

{Supernatural Murder Mystery}

The shocking murder of a professor at San Donorio State College brings the city police to investigate with Campus Police Officer Sarah Ferris acting as college liaison. Sarah's friend, Nico Guardino, a history professor at the college, gets drawn into helping her investigate. As Nico and Sarah struggle to find the murderer, the killing continues.

Drawn inexorably deeper into the investigation, Nico begins having visions and deep feelings of dread he knows somehow connect to the murderer. He feels the connection becoming stronger, but the how and why remain frustratingly unknown even as the visions and feelings become more disturbing.

"A fascinating page turner. Every chapter builds on the next and brings the reader to an unpredictable, satisfying climax. A great (summer) read."

~ Thonie Hevron, award winning author

Publisher: https://www.writers-exchange.com/sin-eater/

You can find ALL our books on our website at:

https://www.writers-exchange.com

All our mysteries:

https://www.writers-exchange.com/category/genres/mystery-thrillers-suspense/

All John's novels:

https://www.writers-exchange.com/john-schembra/

www.ingramcontent.com/pod-product-compliance
Lightning Source LLC
Chambersburg PA
CBHW070555180626
46817CB00005B/1850